HOWDY!

Welcome to the Circle C. My name is Andi Carter. If you are a new reader, here's a quick roundup of my family, friends, and adventures:

I'm a tomboy who lives on a huge cattle ranch near Fresno, California, in the exciting 1880s. I would rather ride my palomino mare, Taffy, than do anything else. I mean well, but trouble just seems to follow me around.

Our family includes my mother, Elizabeth, my ladylike older sister, Melinda, and my three older brothers: Justin (a lawyer), Chad, and Mitch. I love them, but sometimes they treat me like a pest. My father was killed in a ranch accident a few years ago.

In **Long Ride Home**, Taffy is stolen and it's my fault. I set out to find my horse and end up far from home and in a heap of trouble.

In **Dangerous Decision**, I nearly trample my new teacher in a horse race with my friend Cory. Later, I have to make a life-or-death choice.

Next, I discover I'm the only one who doesn't know the Carter **Family Secret**, and it turns my world upside down.

In **San Francisco Smugglers**, a flood sends me to school in the city for two months. My new roommate, Jenny, and I discover that the little Chinese servant-girl in our school is really a slave.

Trouble with Treasure is what Jenny, Cory, and I find when we head into the mountains with Mitch to pan for gold.

And then I may lose my beloved horse, Taffy, if I tell what I saw in **Price of Truth**.

Now saddle up and ride into my latest adventure!

Andi

ANDREA CARTER AND THE

Dangerous Decision

Books by Susan Marlow

Circle C Beginnings
Andi's Pony Trouble
Andi's Indian Summer
Andi's Scary School Days
Andi's Fair Surprise
Andi's Lonely Little Foal
Andi's Circle C Christmas

Circle C Stepping Stones
Andi Saddles Up
Andi Under the Big Top
Andi Lassos Trouble
Andi to the Rescue
Andi Dreams of Gold
Andi Far from Home

Circle C Adventures
Andrea Carter and the Long Ride Home
Andrea Carter and the Dangerous Decision
Andrea Carter and the Family Secret
Andrea Carter and the San Francisco Smugglers
Andrea Carter and the Trouble with Treasure
Andrea Carter and the Price of Truth

Circle C Milestones
Thick as Thieves: An Andrea Carter Book
Heartbreak Trail: An Andrea Carter Book
The Last Ride: An Andrea Carter Book
Courageous Love: An Andrea Carter Book

Goldtown Adventures
Badge of Honor
Tunnel of Gold
Canyon of Danger
River of Peril

EDITION • 2

ANDREA CARTER AND THE

Dangerous Decision

SUSAN K. MARLOW

Kregel
Publications

Andrea Carter and the Dangerous Decision
© 2007, 2018 by Susan K. Marlow

Published by Kregel Publications, a division of Kregel Inc., 2450 Oak Industrial Dr. NE, Grand Rapids, MI 49505.

Scripture quotations are from the King James Version.

ISBN 978-0-8254-4501-9

Printed in the United States of America
19 20 21 22 23 24 25 26 27 / 5 4 3 2

CONTENTS

Chapter One

RACING INTO TROUBLE

SAN JOAQUIN VALLEY, CALIFORNIA, LATE SUMMER, 1880

Twelve-year-old Andrea Carter wrapped her fingers around the reins of her palomino mare, Taffy, and glanced at the rider to her left. Her friend Cory caught her look and grinned. He blew a strand of straw-colored hair from his forehead and tightened his grip on his own mount—a large chestnut gelding.

"I'm gonna beat you today, Andi," he said. "You wait and see. I can't hold my head up in this town anymore—not since the Fourth of July." He leaned over the side of his horse and lowered his voice so only Andi could hear. "You winning that race was nothin' but luck. And I'm gonna prove it."

Andi tossed one of her thick, dark braids behind her shoulder and laughed. "Flash couldn't beat Taffy back in July, and he sure can't beat her now. I don't know why I let you talk me into this."

"Because you like to race as much as I do," Cory shot back. He turned to the dark-haired boy standing on the ground beside the horses. "You ready, Jack?"

Jack Goodwin nodded. He stepped up and balanced himself on the corner of a nearby watering trough. In a loud, clear voice he announced the coming race. "Ladies and gentlemen of Fresno! Step right up for the match race of the season."

A few curious citizens stopped at the sound of the boy's voice. When they realized the race involved nothing more than some idle youths wasting time, they shook their heads and continued down the boardwalk.

"Get on with it, Jack!" A tall, redheaded boy called from several yards away, where a handful of children had gathered to watch. "It's hot out here."

"Aw, keep your shirt on," Jack said. He cupped his hands to his mouth and continued his speech. "This race is for the 1880 fall championship of the county. Riding the sleek chestnut gelding, Flash, is Cory Blake. Cory's pa runs the best livery in the whole valley."

"We know who's riding Flash," another boy yelled.

"I'm puttin' up the prize money," Jack snapped, "so I can do the announcin' any way I like." He raised his voice. "Next to Cory, mounted on the beautiful palomino mare, Taffy, is Andi Carter. Most of you know her folks own the biggest spread around these parts. Finest horseflesh in—"

"Hurry up!" Cory cut in.

"Please, Jack," Andi pleaded. "It's mighty hot."

"Oh, all right." Jack took a deep breath and looked at the riders. "Listen up, you two. This match race is a short loop around town. It starts here, in front of the mercantile. Turn right on Tulare and head outta town 'til you come to Kincaid Vineyards."

Andi opened her mouth to tell Jack she knew the course better than he did, but clamped her jaw shut when he waved an impatient hand in her direction.

"You each snatch a bandana from Ike and head back to town," Jack went on. "Past the schoolhouse. Turn right on J. I'll be here with the prize for the winner." He held up a silver coin. "A dime's worth of anything in my pa's store!" There were cheers and shouts from everyone but Andi and Cory.

Cory rolled his eyes. "We shoulda raced real quiet-like—just you and me—before half the kids in town found out about it," he told Andi.

Andi nodded but didn't answer. Her gaze was fixed on Jack.

He jumped down from the wooden trough, bowed for his audience, and lifted his arm. "Go!" He dropped his arm to his side.

Flash and Taffy leaped forward as one. Shouts of "go, Andi" and "you can beat her, Cory" exploded from the sidelines.

Joy surged through Andi as she nudged her horse into a gallop. Cory was right. She loved to race. There was nothing she would rather do. She didn't care if the sun beat down on her bare head or the wind against her face felt hotter than a blacksmith's forge.

I'm racing, and I'm going to win!

Andi and Cory galloped their horses along J Street. The buildings blurred together into one continuous streak of boards and brick. The Arlington Hotel blended into the hardware store and pharmacy. The Sequoia Restaurant appeared as a smudge of glass and color.

Cory swerved to avoid a buckboard wagon, giving Andi a sudden, unexpected advantage. The red-faced driver stood up and shook his fist. He shouted something Andi couldn't make out, which was probably just as well.

She passed the *Fresno Weekly Expositor* newspaper office and flew around the corner of Tulare Street. The sound of hoofbeats a few feet away spurred her to go even faster. Cory was making up for his unexpected interruption.

Andi knew her friend was partly right about the Fourth of July. Sometimes luck *did* play an important part in a horse race. Cory's gelding wasn't named Flash for nothing. He could very easily gain the lead.

Andi pulled a little farther ahead of her opponent. A finger of worry tickled at the back of her mind. Racing down Tulare Street was risky. She'd have to pass right by her oldest brother's law office. Although Justin was remarkably patient with her most days, Andi doubted he'd approve of her racing through town at breakneck speed.

Before she knew it, the danger of discovery was past and she was heading out of town. Cory galloped up alongside her, gave a cheerful wave, and pulled out ahead. Andi leaned forward and willed Taffy to catch up. They were neck and neck when Kincaid Vineyards came into sight.

Andi reined Taffy to a dead stop in front of a tall, smiling youth. Dust flew everywhere. She snatched the bandana from Ike's hand and drew Taffy around in a sharp pivot. Cory was right beside her on Flash, pleading with his horse to go faster.

"Come on, Taffy," Andi encouraged her mount. "You can beat that ol' gelding any day." The palomino leaped forward, gaining speed on the flat stretch of road that led back into town.

In no time, Andi found herself in the lead, racing down the final stretch of the course. She flew past Davy Cooper, who was sitting on the steps of the two-story schoolhouse, looking bored. He jumped up when he spotted the riders and waved them toward the finish line.

Andi glanced over her shoulder and flashed Cory a smug grin. He'd never catch her now. It was only a few more blocks.

"Andi! Look out!"

Cory's shout sliced through Andi's triumph. She whirled, gasped, and gave the reins a frantic jerk. "Whoa!"

Taffy planted her hooves in the dusty street and nearly sat down. A thick cloud of dust engulfed horse and rider. The mare struggled to regain her footing. She reared up with a frightened whinny.

"Easy, girl," Andi patted her horse's neck. "It's all right. Settle down."

Taffy snorted and tossed her head. Her hooves crashed to the ground only inches from a figure sprawled in the middle of the street. More dust puffed up.

Andi waved the fine powder away from her face and leaned over Taffy's neck for a better view. "Oh *no!*" Her stomach turned over.

A man lay sprawled on his back in the middle of the street. His eyes were squeezed shut, and he'd flung his arms across his head as if to ward off a blow. Two traveling satchels lay open beside him, with books and papers scattered in disarray. A few sheets of paper drifted away on the afternoon breeze.

Andi slid from her saddle and dropped down beside the man. "Are you all right, mister?" Her voice shook. *Oh, please let him be all right*, she silently prayed.

Slowly, as if he couldn't believe he had escaped death, the stranger lowered his arms and opened his eyes. He didn't answer Andi. Instead, he groaned and pulled himself to a sitting position. He seemed dazed.

Cory ran up. "Is he hurt?"

"I don't know. He hasn't said anything yet." Andi laid a hesitant hand on the man's arm. "I'm really sorry, mister. Can I help you up?"

The man blinked and glanced around. Then he narrowed his eyes and pierced Andi with an angry look. "Let me be, you young ruffian!" he snapped, suddenly alert.

Andi jumped up in alarm. The bandana she'd been clutching fell from her hand. "Are you hurt? Do you want me to run for the doctor?"

"Certainly not." The man struggled to his feet and began brushing dust from his well-tailored, dark-blue suit coat. He coughed, took a few cautious steps, and let out a relieved breath. "No bones broken." He glared at Andi. "No thanks to *you*. Is this the usual welcome a stranger receives in this dusty frontier town?"

"It was an a-accident," Andi stammered. She picked up a book, dusted it off, and held it out. "Honest. I didn't mean to run you down. We were racing and I didn't see you—"

"Shame on you!" He snatched the book from Andi's hand and stuffed it into his satchel. "No reputable family would allow their daughter to make a public spectacle of herself—racing through the streets, trampling innocent bystanders." He brought his dust-caked face close to Andi's. "Do you realize I could have been killed?"

Staring into the man's dark, furious eyes, Andi knew he spoke the truth. Another step or two, and Taffy would have run right over the top of him. He might have been killed or crippled. Shivers skittered up her neck. She swallowed her horror and whispered, "Yes, sir. I'm *very* sorry."

The stranger snorted his opinion of Andi's apology. He reached down and began gathering up his scattered papers. "Rowdy, undisciplined youngsters. The sheriff will certainly hear about this."

The sheriff? *Oh no!* "Please, sir, let me help you carry—"

Cory tugged on her sleeve. "I'm getting outta here," he whispered in her ear. "He's not hurt, and he sure doesn't want our help." He edged closer to his horse, pulling Andi along. "We'd best give him a chance to simmer down."

Andi was too frightened to stay behind by herself. Trembling, she mounted Taffy and nudged her mare into a jolting trot.

"Wait! Don't you kids run off!" the stranger bellowed. "We're going to see the sheriff."

Andi watched Cory gallop down the street to safety. Then she pulled Taffy to a stop. Her fingers gripped the reins in indecision. *What should I do? Follow Cory? Try to apologize again and ask the man to leave Sheriff Tate out of this?*

Fear won.

Andi urged Taffy back toward the center of town. She glanced over her shoulder in time to see the man snatch up his satchels, hurry across the street, and disappear inside the schoolhouse. The door slammed shut.

"We're in a heap of trouble," Andi told Cory when she caught up. "We shouldn't have run away. When Sheriff Tate finds out and tells our folks . . ." Her voice trailed away in misery.

Cory slowed his horse to a walk. "He doesn't know who we are. Besides, it was an accident. Give him a day or two and he'll forget all about it."

"You didn't see where he went," Andi said. "I did. He walked into the schoolhouse like he owned it." She gulped. "You don't suppose—"

"Don't even think it." Cory cut her off. "He can't be the new schoolmaster. Your brother wouldn't agree to hire such a bad-tempered man . . . would he?"

Andi didn't know, nor did she care to guess what Justin and the school board had been up to this summer. "But what if he is?"

Cory sighed. "If he is, then you're right. We are in a *heap* of trouble."

Chapter Two

RELUCTANT STUDENT

The first day of school dawned clear, bright, and hot. It was a beautiful morning, but Andi didn't notice. She hadn't noticed much of anything for the past week. She was too busy trying to figure out a way she could avoid the fall term of school—and the new teacher. She had yet to come up with a plan her mother might believe. Her offer to stay home and help put up the fall harvest had fallen on deaf ears.

"I thought offering to peel hundreds of apples was a pretty good idea, Taffy." Andi leaned against her horse and sighed. She'd managed to slip away to the barn after breakfast for an early morning conference with her four-hoofed friend. "But Mother just smiled her I-know-what-you're-thinking smile and said I could help on Saturdays."

She reached into her dress pocket and pulled out a handful of hard, white lumps. "Here. I brought you a treat."

Taffy greedily accepted the offering of sugar and devoured it in one quick bite. She nuzzled Andi's hand, as if hoping to find another treat. When no more tasty white lumps appeared, the mare shook her head. Her ivory mane flew into her owner's face.

Andi brushed it aside. "Oh, Taffy! What if the man I nearly trampled turns out to be the new teacher? I can't face him. I've got to figure out a way to stay home."

Resting her head against Taffy's warm flank, Andi closed her eyes and tried to come up with a plan. She didn't have much time. Any minute now, Justin would be along to drive her to school. *Let's see. I could jump off the barn roof and break an arm or a—*

"It's time to go, Andi."

Andi's eyes flew open. She pushed away from Taffy and faced her brother, who was leaning over the half door of the stall. "So soon? Couldn't I stay home a couple more days?"

"Nope," Justin replied crisply. "Mother made it perfectly clear at breakfast this morning. Let's not go over it again, please."

Andi sighed. It was clear that Justin was in no mood to sympathize with her. She threw her arms around Taffy's neck. "I'll be back this afternoon," she whispered into the mare's ear. "If it's not too hot, we'll go for a long ride."

Andi shuffled out of the stall, latched the bottom half of the door, and followed Justin outside. She blinked when the early morning sunlight struck her face. The day held the promise of unrelenting heat.

She glanced at her family's Spanish-style ranch house. Its white stucco walls glistened in the sun. The red-tiled roof added a splash of color to the brown and barren landscape of a dusty California summer. Huge valley oaks and well-watered gardens surrounded the house and many of the outbuildings, offering a refreshing place to rest and relax during the heat of the day.

To exchange this pleasant setting for the inside of a schoolhouse was the last thing Andi wanted to do today—or any day.

"Mornin' Andi," a cheerful voice called from across the yard. "You look like you're on your way to prison."

Andi shaded her eyes. Her brothers Chad and Mitch stood near the corral, saddling their horses for the day. "I am!" She waved and ran over. "School is the closest thing to prison I can think of, specially on a beautiful morning like this. You should've been at breakfast, when Mother handed down the sentence."

Mitch planted his wide-brimmed hat onto his blond head and winked at her. "What you need is a good lawyer, Sis. Maybe you can ask big brother to appeal your case."

"Not likely. Justin's on Mother's side." Andi stepped onto the bottom railing and peered into the large corral, where the working horses were kept. Half a dozen cowhands were roping and saddling their mounts for the day. They all wore expressions of excitement and expectation.

Andi gazed with longing at the horses. Her brothers and the ranch hands got to ride, while she had to go to school. "Where are you off to?"

"We're going after the rogue stallion," Mitch said. "Chad's bound and determined to get those mares back."

"*What?*" Andi jumped down from the fence. She ignored Justin's loud warning that she would be late for school. "You mean that big, dappled-gray fella who's been running around the range like he owns it?"

"That's the one," Chad said. He finished cinching up his saddle and looked at his sister. His blue eyes flashed. "That maverick has stolen his last mare."

Andi scuffed the dirt. "I sure wish I could go along."

"Sorry, Andi." Chad swung into his saddle. "Maybe some other time."

"Is Melinda going?" she asked with a twinge of envy.

A quiet chuckle relieved Andi's fear that her older sister might accompany the men on their search for the stallion. "Melinda says it's too hot to go chasing after wild horses," Mitch said, pushing back his hat. He leaned toward Andi and lowered his voice. "Justin looks a mite impatient. You'd better go before he comes after you."

Andi tried to hide her disappointment at being left out of what would surely be an exciting day on the ranch. Why had Chad picked *today* of all days to go after the stallion and his stolen band of mares? *No fair!*

She turned away from the corral and kicked a rock. Dust billowed up then settled onto her polished high-top shoes. When she looked up, Justin was shaking his head. She bent down, brushed the dust from her shoes, and hurried over to the buggy.

Her friend Rosa was already waiting in the buggy when Andi climbed in. The Mexican girl's shiny black hair was twisted into a long braid and tied with a red ribbon. Her dark eyes danced with excitement when she greeted Andi with a cheery *buenos días*.

"Hi, Rosa," came Andi's less-than-cheerful reply.

"Are you feeling better about going to school?" Rosa chattered away in Spanish. "I couldn't help overhearing the argument this morning when *Mamá* and I were serving breakfast."

Andi slid over and made room for Justin, who flicked the reins. The horse took off at a lively trot. "No," she replied. "I feel worse than ever. I just learned that Chad and Mitch are going after Whirlwind."

Rosa wrinkled her forehead. "Whirlwind?"

"That's what I named the stallion that showed up a few weeks ago. None of the ranchers will claim him. Nobody knows where he's from, but he's bent on gathering up every mare on the range. I've seen him a couple of times. He's fast as the wind. It sure would be something to go along and watch the boys catch him."

"*Sí,*" Rosa agreed loyally. "I am sure it would be."

Andi squeezed her friend's hand. She knew Rosa had no interest in horses. With a quick glance at her brother, Andi leaned close to Rosa and lowered her voice. "I bet if Father were alive, he'd let me skip a day of school to go after Whirlwind with Chad and Mitch."

"No, he wouldn't," Justin said in English.

Andi opened her mouth to protest, but quickly changed her mind. Arguing with Justin never got her anywhere. He spent his days arguing cases in court and knew all the tricks. She was better off saying nothing at all.

Justin gave the horse another slap of the reins. "What's the matter, Andi? Up until a week ago, you and Rosa were all fired up about the new term. Now you want to back out. That's not like you. Is something wrong?"

Andi shrugged. Something was wrong, all right. It hung over her head like a storm cloud ready to burst. No matter how hard she tried to feel excited about school for Rosa's sake, her stomach churned at the thought of meeting the new teacher.

What if Cory was wrong? What if the schoolmaster had figured out who Andi was? *What if he's waiting in the classroom, ready to pounce the minute I sit down?*

She sat stiffly between Rosa and Justin and clenched her fists in her lap. She didn't feel like talking anymore.

The hour-long trip into Fresno, which on other days flew by, dragged. At long last, Justin pulled up next to the schoolyard and brought the buggy to a halt. "Well, that was the quietest drive into town I've had in a long time." He chuckled.

When Andi didn't respond, Justin said, "Come down to my office after school and I'll give you a ride home."

"*Gracias, Señor* Justin," Rosa said. She jumped lightly from the buggy.

Andi started to follow, but Justin laid a hand on her arm. "Not so fast, young lady."

"Why? What's wrong?" She sat back down and groaned inwardly. Justin was looking at her with his serious, I-want-to-talk-to-you expression. "What about Rosa?" Andi nodded toward her friend, who had moved off a discreet distance to wait. "I shouldn't leave her alone—not on her first day of school."

"Rosa will be just fine," Justin said. "I'd like to know what's troubling *you*. Every time the subject of school has come up this past week, you look ready to run for your life. Why?"

Andi shrugged and stared at her lap. *I should tell him. I really should.* But the words stuck in her throat. "I heard there's a new teacher," she said instead.

Justin nodded. "You heard right. So?"

Andi glanced up at the two-story schoolhouse and made a face. "I don't want a new teacher."

"You begged for a new teacher all last term," Justin reminded her. "I seem to recall hearing about spitballs, peashooters, and Johnny Wilson at least once a week."

Andi frowned. *Me and my big mouth.* She suddenly wished she'd kept her school problems to herself. She could take care of Johnny the bully. But a new schoolmaster? Especially one she'd almost killed?

She shuddered.

"Things are going to be different this year," Justin went on. "We divided the school and hired a new teacher. Miss Hall will continue to instruct the little ones, while Mr. Foster will manage you older, more challenging students upstairs. He assured the school board that he will restore order and discipline—something that's been sorely lacking these past two years."

"A mean, strict schoolmaster? But Justin—"

"Behave yourself, and you won't have a thing to worry about." Justin tweaked one of Andi's long, dark curls. "Don't fret, honey. Mr. Foster seems like a fair and honest man. Perhaps a little more straitlaced than you and your friends are used to, but he's from back East. He'll learn our ways, and you'll adjust."

Andi wasn't so sure about that. A city slicker trying to manage a classroom full of ranchers' and farmers' kids? He was in for a surprise.

"Mr. Foster has a daughter," Justin said.

That brought Andi up short. "A daughter?"

"Two, actually. I met the girl your age when Mr. Foster came by the office to sign his contract. She seems like a nice, quiet young lady. Perhaps you could show her a warm California welcome." He paused, as if expecting a response.

"Uh, sure, Justin."

Justin sighed. "Listen, Andi. Mr. Foster left his position as head-master of a prominent school back East to move his family out here.

It's been a difficult adjustment, so I don't want you giving the man any trouble."

Andi cringed. She never purposely gave *anyone* trouble. Trouble just seemed to follow her around—like last Saturday's disaster.

Justin was still talking. "Mr. Foster's going to have his hands full enough as it is, without you adding to his problems." He pulled a copy of the *Expositor* from his leather satchel and handed it to her. "Take a look at the story near the bottom of the page. It's not the welcome I would have chosen."

Andi took the newspaper and began reading. "'From Gerald Foster, our new schoolmaster, we learn that quite an excitement was stirred up the other day down in front of the grammar school. It appears that a couple of young rowdies gave the teacher an unforgettable welcome to our fair city by nearly stampeding him with their horses. Mr. Foster has taken the matter up with the sheriff and hopes to quickly identify and bring the offenders before Judge Morrison on a charge of—'"

Andi caught her breath. "Malicious mischief!" It was a serious charge. She tossed the paper onto Justin's lap. She couldn't read any more.

This is getting worse and worse. I have to tell him.

Justin folded the paper. "I told Sheriff Tate that my money's on the Hollister kids. They're a wild bunch and wouldn't think twice before tearing through town on their horses or roughing up the new schoolmaster." He shook his head. "And the Hollister kids are the least of his worries. There's Johnny Wilson—"

"It wasn't Sadie and Zeke Hollister," Andi blurted, before she changed her mind.

"Oh?" Justin raised his eyebrows in interest. "You know who it was?"

Andi nodded. "It was . . . Cory and me." She swallowed. "Mostly it was me."

"No!"

"It was an accident." Her words rushed out. "Cory and I were racing, and I didn't see him. Honest, I didn't. It happened so fast. He came out of nowhere. But you should've seen Taffy! She can stop on a dime. And a good thing too. Not a hoof touched Mr. Foster."

She paused at the dismay written all over Justin's face. "Well," she offered in a tiny voice, "it could have been worse."

Justin sat motionless, staring at the newspaper on his lap.

"Justin?" Andi whispered. "Say something."

"What do you want me to say? The *Expositor* made light of the incident, but it's no joke. You've certainly gotten yourself into a fix *this* time."

Andi hung her head. "I know, and I'm sorry. But I have an idea. Let me wait in your office while you write up some fancy legal papers to convince Mr. Foster to drop those malicious mischief charges." She looked up. "You can do that, can't you?"

"Not today, I'm afraid. Preparing Jed Hatton's defense is taking all of my time. The trial's only a few weeks away."

Andi sighed her impatience. "He killed Mr. Slater, Justin. He's just a dirty old drifter who—"

"Who is innocent until proven guilty." Justin frowned. "Don't listen to gossip, Andi. It's dangerous and stirs folks up. Next thing you know they turn into a lynch mob."

When Andi didn't reply, Justin stepped out of the buggy. "It's time to go." He reached out a helping hand.

The big-brother talk was over.

Andi took Justin's hand and hopped to the ground. "What about Mr. Foster? I can't go to school until this is settled."

"Oh yes you can, and you will." Justin climbed back into the buggy and lifted the reins. "If I find the time, I'll see what I can do to help you out, but for now you'll just have to make the best of it."

He chirruped to the horse and drove away, leaving Andi standing in the street.

Chapter Three

THE NEW TEACHER

Y ou look terrible," Rosa remarked when Andi joined her. "What did *Señor* Justin say to you?" She shaded her eyes and watched the buggy turn the corner onto J Street. "Are you in trouble again?"

"The worst ever." Andi took a deep breath and told her friend about her encounter with the new teacher.

Rosa's dark eyes widened. *"¡Qué terrible!"* she said when Andi had finished. "What will you do?"

"I don't know." Andi crossed the schoolyard and paused near the bottom of the steps. There was no sense going into class before the bell rang. Perhaps if she stayed hidden in the crowd, she would go unnoticed by the teacher.

She glanced around the yard. No one seemed eager to enter the schoolhouse. An impromptu game of baseball was in full swing on the far side of the building. The yard in front was filled with jump ropes and colorful skirts.

Andi didn't feel like joining them. Instead, she settled herself on the bottom step and cupped her chin in her hands.

"When do we go into the classroom?" Rosa gazed up at the bell tower above the double doors.

Andi set aside her own troubles for a moment and laid a reassuring hand on Rosa's arm. "When the bell rings." She smiled. "Don't worry. You're so smart. You'll catch up fast in your lessons. After all, haven't I been teaching you English all summer? And reading too?"

Rosa nodded.

Andi paused and chewed her lip. "Just remember one thing."

"What is that, *mi amiga*?"

Andi pointed to the entrance at the top of the steps. "The minute we step through those doors, we can't speak Spanish."

Rosa sighed. "English is so difficult. Maybe I can speak Spanish with you, if I speak quietly?"

Andi shook her head. "You can't, or we'll both be in trouble. Miss Hall is strict about everybody speaking proper English, and I'm sure Mr. Foster will be just as strict."

A sudden stab of uncertainty made Andi pause. Justin had assured her many times this summer that Rosa could attend school, but he warned her that it might not be easy. Many students would not be able to overlook the fact that Rosa was Mexican. Andi had clenched her fists and shouted "unfair," but she knew Justin was telling her the truth.

"Don't forget," she told Rosa. "You must speak English."

The school bell rang. Andi jumped up, grabbed Rosa's hand, and yanked her out of the way. A crowd of noisy boys swarmed up the front steps and disappeared through the double doors.

"Let's wait for the girls," Andi told Rosa. She waved to her friends Rachel and Maggie, who hurried over.

"Hi, Andi." Rachel's blue eyes sparkled with curiosity. "Is this Rosa?" When Andi nodded, Rachel gave the Mexican girl a tentative smile. "I'm glad Andi talked you into coming to school."

Maggie linked an arm with Rosa. "I'm glad too. Our class can never have too many girls. I hope you stay all term."

A warm glow spread through Andi. Her friends had welcomed Rosa just like she'd hoped they would.

"*Graci*—thank you," Rosa said. Together, the girls climbed the wide steps and entered the schoolhouse.

"Mornin', Andi," Cory called out. He was leaning against the wall at the bottom of a narrow staircase that led up to the classroom. He folded his arms across his chest and grinned. "Ready to meet the new teacher?"

Andi stopped short. For a few minutes, she'd forgotten her own anxiety. Now it returned in full force. She looked at Rosa. "Go up with Rachel and Maggie. I'll be along in a minute."

When the girls were out of sight, Andi whirled on Cory. "How can you be so cocksure of yourself?" she said in a low voice. "Don't you know Mr. Foster's got the sheriff looking all over town for the kids who trampled him?"

Cory dug his hands deep into his pockets. "'Course I know. I saw the paper. But I heard he thinks it's the Hollister kids. I've got a notion to let him go on thinking that."

"That's fine for *you*," Andi said hotly. "All boys in overalls look pretty much alike. But what about *me*?"

"He'll never guess it was you. You're all slicked up like a proper girl today. He's looking for a wild ruffian in faded riding clothes, not a pretty girl in a new dress"—he chuckled—"who also just happens to be a Carter." He winked. "You've got nothin' to worry about."

Andi's spirits rose. Perhaps there was a kernel of truth in Cory's silly talk. She did look different from the dusty and frightened girl who'd nearly run over the new schoolmaster the week before. Maybe he wouldn't recognize her, and the whole regrettable incident could fade away like a bad dream.

She brushed her dark tangles behind her shoulder and gave Cory a heartfelt smile. "You sure know how to cheer a person up."

"Happy to help," Cory said. "Now, take a look at this." He fumbled around in his pocket and drew out the slender thread of a black and red snake. Its forked tongue flicked a warning. "It's for you. The first day of school wouldn't be the same if I didn't bring you a present." He held it out.

Andi shook her head and backed away. "Not this year, Cory. I don't want any snakes in my desk—today or any day. Justin says the new teacher is nothing like Miss Hall. If he catches you or me with a snake or a frog or any crawly bug, it'll be more than the corner for us. You better get rid of it."

"Get rid of this swell little fella?" Cory sounded shocked. "Not on your life."

Andi shrugged. "Suit yourself." She turned her back on him and scurried up the steps.

Cory laughed and hurried after her.

When Andi reached the top of the stairs, she entered the classroom and glanced around. Mr. Foster was nowhere in sight. She let out a grateful sigh and relaxed. Then she looked for her friends. She spotted them near the center of the room, giggling together. Rosa waved.

"We saved you a seat," Rachel called over the commotion.

Andi grinned and began to wind her way through the crowd.

She was brought to a sudden halt when one of the boys in a far back seat slammed his boot heel down on a desk, blocking her way. "I hear your brother's defending that killer, Jed Hatton," he said. "Now, why in the world would he do such a fool thing?"

Andi rushed to Justin's defense. "Not that it's any of *your* business, Johnny Wilson, but Justin says Jed's innocent." She gave him her fiercest look. "Move."

Johnny rolled his eyes and shifted his leg barely enough to let her pass. He grabbed for her hair, but Andi was too fast. She slipped out of his reach and hurried between the desks. Snickers from Johnny's friends followed her up the aisle.

Andi bristled. Maybe there was some sense in having a mean, strict teacher after all, if he could tame the classroom bullies. She turned and glared at the boys before sliding into the seat Rachel had saved for her. "Thanks."

It was one of the best seats in class—far enough away to be out from under the schoolmaster's critical gaze, yet not too close to become a target for mean-spirited pranks from the boys in the back. Rosa slid in beside her.

Cory threw himself into an empty desk across from Andi. "I saw Johnny teasing you. I'd like to knock him clear into the next county."

"You tried that last term, remember?" Andi said. "He gave you a black eye and a bloody nose. He's older than you, and bigger."

"Maybe I should give him a little surprise." Cory wiggled his hand in his pocket.

Andi gasped. "You can't. Johnny will kill it for sure."

"Well then, since you feel so sorry for my new pet"—he drew the snake from his pocket—"you'd best keep him safe for me."

"No, Cory!"

Too late. Cory lifted the lid of Andi's desk, dropped the snake inside, and slammed the lid shut with a *bang*. "You take good care of him now, y'hear? By the way—welcome back to school." He darted down the aisle and plopped into the seat next to Jack Goodwin.

Rosa's hand flew to her mouth.

"I'm sorry, Rosa," Andi whispered in Spanish. "Don't worry. I'll get rid of it at recess. It's just that Cory's brought me a snake on the first day of school ever since I can remember. It's a tradition."

"A strange and horrifying tradition," Rosa muttered between her fingers.

The second bell rang, and the new schoolmaster entered the class-room.

Andi's eyes widened. She never would have guessed this was the same man she had nearly trampled. No dust covered his neatly pressed dark pants and waistcoat. No fear showed in his stern face. Not a hair was misplaced, not a button undone.

He walked up the aisle with long, purposeful strides, turned, and stood in front of his desk. "My name is Mr. Foster," he announced. "I am your new schoolmaster."

The pupils fell silent.

"The school board has charged me with bringing order to this classroom. They warned me of your rowdiness. I am here to see that you are rowdy no longer."

Andi chanced a quick glance at the back of the room. Every boy sat ramrod straight, gazes locked on Mr. Foster. Even Johnny Wilson looked subdued.

Mr. Foster took his place behind his desk and continued his speech. "You will conduct yourselves as ladies and gentlemen at all times—inside the classroom and after hours. Truthfulness, honesty, punctuality, cleanliness, and kindness to others will be the ambition of our class, along with the highest standards of academic achievement. To achieve these goals, I have drawn up a list of rules."

He raised his voice. "Virginia, if you would bring me the list?"

Forty heads twisted around. A girl about Andi's age stood near the top of the stairs, surveying the classroom. She clutched a paper in her hand.

"This is my daughter Virginia," Mr. Foster said. "She will be joining us this term. You will find her to be a fine pupil and a capable tutor, should any of you need help in your studies. I trust you will do your best to make her feel welcome." He motioned her forward.

Virginia Foster glided to the front of the classroom, handed her father the paper, and turned to face her new classmates. She curtsied. "I'm pleased to make your acquaintance," she said in a low, soft voice.

Her greeting was met with absolute silence.

"Do none of you know how to make your manners?" Mr. Foster asked, clearly astonished.

Andi knew how, but she didn't want to bring attention to herself. She quietly studied Virginia instead. *This must be the girl Justin wants me to offer a friendly welcome to.*

The teacher's daughter was a thin, pale girl, with hair so white it looked like a fluff of clouds around her head. Her eyebrows were nearly invisible. Only her eyes showed color—the same striking gray as her father's. She wore a simple frock of yellow and green calico.

Walter Hancock's drawl pulled Andi's attention back to class. "We ain't much for fancy ways around here." He grinned. "Howdy, Ginny."

Virginia's cheeks flushed a delicate pink.

Mr. Foster sucked in a breath. "Surely the class can do better than that."

A few girls curtsied and said hello, but most of the pupils just stared. Andi felt a twinge of embarrassment for her friends' poor manners, but she stayed put.

Mr. Foster motioned Virginia to find a seat. He cleared his throat. "Your attention, please. I will begin by reading the rules. Later, I will post them on the back wall."

"Next to the stairs," Andi whispered to Rosa. "That way we can't help but see them every time we go in and out."

Mr. Foster quickly went over the rules, dropped the paper onto his desktop, and looked at his class. "I will also manage this class by assigning seats. The school board drew up a list of names and helped me place you in seats that would be most beneficial to your learning."

The room exploded into groans and complaints.

"No fair!"

"Miss Hall never—"

"Silence!" The teacher picked up a ruler and slammed it down on his desk. "I will tolerate no disrespect toward the school board's decision in this matter. Listen as I call your names and direct you to your seats."

The next few minutes erupted into noisy chaos.

Virginia looked bewildered at the confusion, but it wasn't long before she gathered herself together and moved up the aisle. She stopped beside Andi. "My father assigned me this seat."

Andi exchanged a long, meaningful look with Virginia and said nothing.

"Didn't you hear me?" the girl snapped. "This is my seat."

Andi stood up and beckoned Rosa to do the same. All of a sudden, offering Virginia a warm California welcome was the furthest thing from Andi's mind. Miss Virginia Foster might look and act like a correct, gentle little lady on the outside, but Andi saw a spark of something else flash from behind those dark-gray eyes.

She sure figured out how to wrangle the best seat in the classroom. "Let's go, Rosa."

She watched Rachel and Maggie take their seats in front of Johnny Wilson and Walter Hancock. Too bad for her friends. Johnny was the biggest bully in the—

"I've chosen a seat especially for you."

Andi spun and faced Mr. Foster. "For me?"

He nodded. "Do you think I don't recognize you, Sadie Hollister, as the ill-mannered girl who nearly ended my life the other day?"

"Sadie *Hollister*?" Andi's heart sank. So much for Cory's silly notion that she wouldn't be recognized.

"Yes." He led Andi to the front of the room and thrust her into the first desk. "You will sit right here, where I can keep an eye on you. Now, where is your unruly brother?"

Jack Goodwin snickered.

"I'm not Sadie," Andi said. "The Hollisters hardly ever come to school."

Andi couldn't remember the last time she'd seen her sheepherder friend from the hills. The two girls used to play together all the time, but they'd grown apart over the last year.

A look of confusion replaced the teacher's frown. "I was told it was most likely the Hollister youngsters who . . ." His voice trailed off, and the scowl returned. "Well, then! What *is* your name?"

Andi swallowed. "Andrea Carter."

"Carter . . . Carter . . ." The schoolmaster scanned the class list. His frown deepened. "Carter as in Justin Carter, one of our school trustees?"

Andi nodded. "He's my brother."

"I'm sure you make your family very proud."

31

Mr. Foster's mocking words felt like a slap to Andi's face. Her cheeks burned.

"It appears that you're sitting over there, along with a Mexican girl." He pointed to the double seat in front of Cory. "You are not starting out the term well, young lady—if I can call you that. Don't think for one minute I've forgotten the way you welcomed me to your town."

"No, sir. It won't happen again."

"I dare say it won't. Now, go find your seat before I forget your name is Carter and punish you as you deserve."

"Yes, sir." Andi jumped up and scurried across the room. She sat down, grateful to be away from Mr. Foster's harsh words. She waved Rosa over. "You're sitting with me."

Rosa slipped into her seat and regarded Andi with dark, troubled eyes. "I do not like this American school, *mi amiga*. The schoolmaster speaks too fast, with words I do not understand. Perhaps it is better if I stay home."

Andi gripped Rosa's hand. "Please stay, Rosa. It will get better." She managed a grin. "It can't get much worse."

A shriek of pure terror suddenly came from the middle of the room. Andi caught her breath at the frightening sound.

Before she could discover what was wrong, Cory jabbed her between the shoulder blades. "I think the teacher's kid just found your welcome-back gift."

Chapter Four

FROM BAD TO WORSE

Andi didn't think anyone could run as fast as Virginia Foster ran during the next six seconds. She tore down the aisle and scrambled onto the top of the teacher's desk. There she cowered, screaming.

Andi watched in astonishment. For a dainty, quiet young lady, Virginia sure could holler.

The class burst into shouts of laughter. Cory fell from his chair, holding his stomach. He howled with glee at this unexpected distraction.

"What happened?"

"Did you see that?"

"What's going on?"

"Silence!" Mr. Foster bellowed. He lifted his ruler and brought it crashing down against an empty front-row desk. The laughter died away until Virginia's wail was the only sound in the classroom.

The teacher reached up and gathered Virginia into his arms. "Hush, daughter. There is never a good reason to act with such an unladylike display." He lowered her to the floor. "Tell me what happened."

Virginia's shrieks subsided into hysterical sobbing. "There's a . . . huge creature . . . slithering in my desk," she exclaimed between sobs. "It's horrible." She choked back a cry and covered her face with her hands. "How could anyone be so cruel?"

"Virginia, calm yourself. You'll become ill," Mr. Foster said.

He left his daughter and marched up the aisle to the recently abandoned desk. Flinging open the lid, he reached inside and lifted out the baby snake. It writhed helplessly in the teacher's grasp. "I do not believe 'huge creature' accurately describes this tiny reptile, daughter."

At the sight of the snake, half a dozen girls leaped from their seats and began screeching. The boys doubled over with renewed laughter.

Andi laughed right along with them. "I told you it would get better," she whispered to Rosa between giggles.

Rosa did not laugh. "This is not good, *mi amiga*. That poor girl is truly frightened, and I don't blame her." She paused. "The snake was in *your* desk."

Andi swallowed her laughter as Rosa's words hit home. All of a sudden, the situation did not seem very funny.

To make matters worse, Virginia crumpled onto the floor in a heap, striking her head on the edge of the teacher's desk.

"Virginia fainted!" Davy Cooper shouted above the clamor.

The classroom grew still.

Mr. Foster opened a window and gave the snake a toss. Then he crossed to where his daughter lay unconscious. "Wake up, Virginia." He patted her cheek. "The snake is gone."

Virginia's eyes flew open.

Mr. Foster helped her to her feet and led her back to her desk. "Sit down now. It's all over."

Virginia collapsed into her seat. "Please send for Mother. I'm ill. I feel faint."

"Oooh!" Patricia Newton squealed. "Your forehead's bleeding!"

Virginia's fingers flew to her head. The sight of her own blood sent her into another round of hysterical crying.

Mr. Foster drew a handkerchief from his vest pocket. "It's nothing more than a scratch, daughter. Take this." He pressed the cloth to Virginia's forehead and guided her shaking hand to hold it firmly in place. "Now, stop crying."

When Virginia's sobs had quieted to muffled whimpering, the teacher returned to the front of the room. He picked up his ruler. "Who put the snake in my daughter's desk?"

No one spoke. No one moved.

Mr. Foster tapped his ruler against his palm. "I want a name."

Andi's gaze was riveted on the ruler in Mr. Foster's hand. Chad and Mitch had told her stories about teachers who hit their students for the smallest offense, but she never dreamed she'd see it for herself. Miss Hall was the gentlest of souls. Her punishments never went beyond a trip to the corner or a note sent home.

The snake had been found in Andi's desk, but every pupil except Virginia knew it belonged to Cory. *I bet this is the last snake he ever brings to class.* Andi's throat tightened in sympathy for her friend.

"*That* girl knows who did it." Virginia pointed at Andi.

Andi's heart skipped a beat. *"What?"*

"She was sitting in this desk before I was." Virginia hiccupped and rubbed the tears from her eyes. "She knew about the snake but didn't tell me." She hiccupped again. "Perhaps she put it there herself."

"No, sir." Andi shook her head. "I didn't put it there."

"Then who did?"

Andi didn't answer. Mr. Foster would have to find the culprit without her help.

The teacher sighed. "Very well. Did you know the snake was in your desk?"

Andi squirmed. "Yes, sir. But in all the confusion of switching seats, I forgot about it." She took a deep breath. "I didn't mean to leave it there. Besides, it's just a little snake—nothing to get all fired up about."

The schoolmaster narrowed his eyes. "Do you call terrifying a new student with a cruel joke and then laughing over it nothing to get all fired up about?"

"No, sir. I'm sorry, sir." She turned to Virginia. "I'm sorry you got hurt, Virginia."

35

Virginia buried her head in her arms and refused to look at Andi. Her father's blood-smeared handkerchief lay on the desk beside her.

Mr. Foster picked up his list. "Miss Carter, these rules forbid bringing live creatures of any sort into this classroom. The punishment is four licks of the switch for boys, four licks of the ruler for girls." He dropped the paper and picked up his ruler. "Pass to the front."

Andi gulped. "I didn't bring the snake into class, Mr. Foster."

"Then who did?" When Andi made no reply, he motioned her forward.

By the time she reached Mr. Foster's desk, Andi was near panic. The teacher towered over her, his lips set in a firm, disapproving line. "Put out your palm."

"Wait!" A white-faced Cory sprang from his seat. "Andi's not to blame. *I* put the snake in her desk. She told me not to, but I did it anyway."

It's about time! Andi wanted to shout at Cory. She felt weak with relief.

"That's right," Jack added. "Cory's always one for bringin' in snakes an' spiders and such."

"It's not Andi's fault," Rachel said.

Mr. Foster's frown deepened. "I'm afraid your confessions come too late. Miss Carter's punishment will serve as a lesson to all of you that I am not a schoolmaster to be trifled with."

"But, sir!" Cory argued. "It's not fair to punish her for something I did."

"Then next time do not delay. Speak up at once." He raised his ruler and brought it down against Andi's palm with a loud *whack*.

Blinking back tears of anger and humiliation, Andi returned to her seat in disgrace. The four licks didn't hurt nearly as much as the shame of being punished unjustly—especially on the first day of school.

"I'm sorry I waited to speak up," Cory apologized, leaning over Andi's shoulder. "I truly didn't think he'd punish you. Not the first

FROM BAD TO WORSE

day. Not with Justin on the school board." He shook his head. "I botched things up pretty bad, but I'll make it up to you. I promise. Don't be sore for keeps."

Andi shrugged Cory's apology away. She could never stay mad at him for longer than a few minutes, no matter how hard she tried.

Her anger with Mr. Foster was a different matter, however. She'd seen the gleam in his eyes just before he whacked her palm. She was certain he was using the snake incident as an excuse to punish her for nearly trampling him the other day. Why else would he be so ridiculously unfair?

Justin told me Mr. Foster was a fair and honest man. Ha!

She returned her attention to the front of the classroom when Mr. Foster began speaking. He held a Bible in his hands. "The board has determined that each school day will begin with a selection from the Holy Scriptures." He made a great show of leafing through the pages of the Bible. When he found the place, he cleared his throat and began reading, "'Blessed is the man that walketh not in the counsel of the ungodly, nor standeth in the way of sinners, nor . . .'"

Andi listened in disappointment while Mr. Foster droned his way through Psalm 1. He read the passage without feeling, as if it were nothing more than a dictionary entry. Andi knew the passage by heart, so she shut her ears to his voice and sent up a quick prayer that she could finish the rest of the day without any more clashes with the schoolmaster.

"Begin your lessons," Mr. Foster directed when he had finished. "I will place you into classes when I hear you recite."

Andi opened her reader and tried to concentrate on her lesson, but her thoughts kept returning to her earlier humiliation. A wave of longing for the familiar, cheerful confusion of Miss Hall's classroom rose up inside her. Miss Hall would never have asked who put the snake in the desk. She knew. She *always* knew. Cory would have been marched quickly to his usual corner without any fuss.

Andi slumped in her seat. Right now she should be happily

acquainting Rosa with the joys of learning. She'd looked forward to helping her friend adjust to a strange school and new customs.

Not anymore. Now she would be trapped for seven hours each day in a classroom with a teacher whose word was law. He held an unfair grudge against her on account of her recklessness the other day, and he didn't appear willing to forgive her anytime soon.

Worse, it looked like she'd ruined any chance of making friends with Virginia. No doubt her father would forbid his daughter to associate with such a brash and reckless girl as Andrea Carter. *He's probably afraid I'll run her over with my horse or torment her with another snake or something.*

She hazarded a peek at Virginia, who glanced back at the same time. Andi tried her best I'm-really-sorry-can-we-be-friends smile, but Virginia pursed her lips into an expression that told Andi she was *not* interested.

Andi sighed. It was going to be a long term.

Chapter Five

THE ACCIDENT

T he teacher knows you are in the tree," Rosa said one noon recess two weeks later. She shaded her eyes and looked up.

Andi stood motionless on one of the oak's huge, spreading branches and glanced down at her friend. "Are you sure?"

Rosa nodded. "Come down," she pleaded in her slow, careful English. "Please."

"In a minute," Andi replied. "I've just . . . about"—she held her breath—"got it. Here. Catch." She dropped a heavy canning jar into Rosa's waiting hands. Then, branch by branch, Andi lowered herself to the ground.

A handful of excited little girls swarmed her.

Seven-year-old Emily threw her arms around Andi's waist. "I knew you could do it." She gave Andi an adoring grin. "You can catch most anything, I bet—spiders, snakes, frogs, and the like."

Andi untangled Emily's arms from around her waist. "Just about," she agreed. "Would you like me to catch you a spider sometime? I know where there're some specially big, hairy tarantulas. They move around a lot this time of year."

Emily shrieked. "No! Ew. I don't like spiders—big or little."

Andi smiled and reached for the jar in Rosa's hand. Inside, an orange and black monarch fluttered. "Here's your butterfly."

Emily clutched her prize to her chest. "Thank you, Andi." She and the other little girls skipped away in a flurry of colorful skirts and pinafores.

Andi brushed leaves and twigs from her dress and looked up at the second-story schoolhouse window. The teacher stood behind the glass with his arms locked in front of his chest. He was frowning, as usual.

Rosa was right. Caught again. "I'll be copying lines today," she said. "You wait and see. I can't turn around without Mr. Foster finding fault with me for something. I think it's his way of reminding me that he hasn't forgotten about the trampling."

She went back to brushing her skirt clean. "What I can't figure out is how he catches me so often. He can't be everywhere at once. How could he be at the window at exactly the same time I was catching that butterfly for Emily? I wasn't in the tree longer than four or five minutes."

"I think he has help," Rosa said. "Look."

Andi glanced up. Her jaw tightened. Mr. Foster had disappeared from view, but the second-story classroom window was by no means empty. Virginia stood behind the glass, watching the activity in the schoolyard.

Andi turned away. "You're right, Rosa. It looks like Virginia's running to her father with tales about me. I've tried to be nice to her, but she's not about to forget Cory's snake—even though that wasn't even my fault." She shook her head. "This term's getting worse by the day."

Just then a small, curly-haired boy raced up. "Hey, Andi!" He yanked on her sleeve. "Why did you catch Emily a swell butterfly like that?"

Andi put her hands on her hips. "Three reasons, Toby. First, she asked me to catch it. Second, she gave me the jar. And third"—she jabbed a finger into the little boy's chest—"she won't stick it with a pin and mount it on a piece of wood when she's done with it. She'll let it go."

"Aw, Andi," Toby grumbled, "that's a waste of a good butterfly."

"What do you want?" Andi asked.

He grinned. "Cory sent me to fetch you to come play ball. Seth hurt his arm last inning, so Cory needs a new player for his team."

"Can't he ask Ollie?"

Toby shook his head. "Cory wants *you*. He says you play near as good as any boy on the team." He grabbed Andi's hand. "C'mon. He told me not to come back without you."

Andi paused. Playing baseball was nearly as much fun as racing her horse. Miss Hall had always looked the other way when Andi joined the boys in their ball games. Mother had never said no, and Andi had never given either her former teacher or her mother any reason to withdraw the privilege.

But now? It was a new school year and a new teacher. Mr. Foster would probably disapprove, but he was nowhere in sight. Neither was his daughter. The noon hour was just about over. What could it hurt? She looked at Rosa.

"I think maybe you will be copying many, *many* lines if you do this," her friend said.

Andi shook off her uneasiness and made her decision. "It will be worth it." She followed Toby to the dusty field behind the school-house.

"Over here, Andi!" Cory grabbed her hand and pulled her into the clump of players waiting their turn to bat. "You're just in time. You're taking Seth's place, and you're up next."

"Batter up!" Jack Goodwin yelled from his catcher's position. "We haven't got all day."

Andi grabbed the bat and headed for the rough square of wood that served as home plate. She eyed the pitcher and scowled.

Johnny Wilson scowled back. He loosened the collar of his fancy shirt and kicked aside the expensive suit coat lying in a heap at his feet. "No girls." He planted his meaty fists on his hips.

Andi let out an impatient breath. Johnny always griped about no girls playing ball.

"What do you care?" Cory shot back. "She's not on your team."

Johnny glared at Andi for a moment, then shrugged. "Suit yourself. But I'm not going easy on her just cuz she's a girl."

"Who's asking you to?" Andi shouted. "Play ball!"

Johnny's expression twisted into a sneer. With a snap of his wrist, he hurled the ball toward home plate. Andi swung. The ball flew past her and landed in the catcher's bare hands with a loud *smack*.

"Strike one!" Jack tossed the ball back to the pitcher and rubbed his palms against his britches.

Johnny snickered. "Too fast for you, Andi?" Before she could respond, he threw the ball a second time.

Andi clenched her teeth and swung. The ball cracked against the bat and popped up, back over her head. It bounced three times and rolled to a stop near the corner of the schoolhouse.

"Foul ball." Jack grinned at her before going after the ball. "Cory's team's gonna lose if you go on hitting like that."

"Keep quiet," Andi muttered. She swung the bat to her shoulder.

Johnny threw the next pitch.

Andi swung. The ball flew up and over her head.

"Another foul," Jack grumbled. "I'm tired of chasing your—" He gasped. *"Oh no!"*

Andi spun around just in time to see the ball smash into the schoolhouse's second-story window. An earsplitting *crack* was followed by the tinkling of a thousand pieces of glass.

Then silence.

Andi dropped the bat and stared at the window in stunned disbelief. *What have I done?* Her throat turned dry. Fear clutched her from the inside out.

The other ballplayers looked just as frightened. They crowded around Andi, wide-eyed and speechless. Johnny broke the silence with a nervous laugh. "Great hit, Andi." He came and stood beside her. "Maybe next time you'll hit ol' Foster right on the head."

Nobody laughed.

The door to the schoolhouse flew open. The schoolmaster raced down the back steps, followed more slowly by a pale-faced Miss Hall.

"The classroom is a shambles." Mr. Foster came to a stop in the middle of the field. His face was filled with rage. "My daughter came close to being seriously injured. Who is responsible for this act?"

No one answered. By now, every pupil, young and old, had been drawn to the ball field. Some of the smaller children were crying. When they saw Miss Hall, they ran over and clutched her skirt.

Mr. Foster looked at the crying children and the bewildered Miss Hall. He took a deep breath and composed himself. "This does not concern any of your scholars, Miss Hall," he said in a calmer tone. "The noon recess is over. Please take the younger ones inside."

The rest of the little children ran to Miss Hall like frightened chicks scurrying for their mother. She guided them back into the schoolhouse, out of sight of the angry Mr. Foster.

The schoolmaster returned his attention to the older boys. They were clumped together in a nervous group. "Who broke the window?"

The boys shuffled their feet and stared at the ground. Even Johnny Wilson looked uncomfortable. He slung his suit coat over his shoulder and studied the tops of his shoes.

Mr. Foster turned to the two dozen girls who stood several yards away. "Do any of you young ladies know who destroyed the window?"

If they knew, none of the girls were saying. They huddled together and didn't respond.

The schoolmaster turned back to the ballplayers. "Your silence is unacceptable. If no one confesses, then every boy here will be punished."

Andi's heart pounded against the inside of her chest like a mighty fist. Sweat trickled down the back of her neck. *I have to own up.* Nobody would turn her in—not even Johnny Wilson.

If I don't speak up, all the boys will be punished. It will be my fault. She swallowed and opened her mouth, but no words came out.

"I did it." Cory's confession drew startled looks from the other boys. There were gasps from the girls, including Andi. Cory picked up the bat and handed it to Mr. Foster. "It was an accident. I'll clean it up right away." He turned to Andi, warning her with a look to keep quiet.

"Mr. Blake. I might have known." He grasped the boy's ear. Cory yelped. "Come along with me, boy. You will feel the switch today."

The switch! Andi groaned. She wanted to run after the teacher and set things straight, but her legs felt like jelly.

Davy kicked a rock. "Cory's sure gonna get it."

"Cory's a fool," Johnny said. He joined the small crowd making its way back to the schoolhouse. "I wouldn't take the blame for no girl."

"You gonna tell the teacher?" Ike asked. He gave Andi a worried look.

Johnny shook his head. "If Cory wants to act all noble and take Andi's thrashing, I reckon that's his business."

"None of us'll tell," Davy assured Andi. He spread his arms wide to include the girls who had joined them. "One thrashing today is plenty." There were nods all around. "We'll all stick by you, Andi."

The loyalty of her friends should have cheered her, but it didn't. Instead, she felt miserable for not speaking up.

The students climbed the stairs in uneasy silence. They entered the classroom in time to see the teacher administering the last of several well-aimed strokes to Cory's backside.

Andi cringed at the sight and quickly found her seat.

"Clean up this mess, Mr. Blake."

"Yes, sir," Cory replied stiffly. He headed to the back of the room for the broom.

"The rest of you should check for glass splinters before seating yourselves," Mr. Foster said. "Fourth Reader Class, gather your books and come forward for recitation."

"Excuse me."

Virginia's voice turned Mr. Foster's attention to his daughter. "Yes? What is it, Miss Foster?"

Virginia stood beside her desk and curtsied. "Father, I think I need to tell you something."

"Does it concern your recitation?"

Virginia shook her head. "No, sir. It concerns the broken window." She took a deep breath. "The truth is, Cory Blake did not break it."

Mr. Foster narrowed his eyes. "Are you certain?"

"Yes, sir. If you recall, I stayed indoors during the noon hour. I was watching the ball game from over there." She pointed to the far side of the classroom. "The ball crashed through the window not ten feet from where I was standing. Andrea Carter was holding the bat."

Mr. Foster turned a disbelieving look on Andi. "*You* broke the window?"

"*I* broke it," Cory insisted from the back of the room. "Ask anybody."

"Wait!" Andi jumped to her feet. Cory's lie would only dig the two of them into deeper trouble. It was time to make things right. "Virginia's right. I broke it. But it was an accident, just like Cory said." She swallowed the lump that had suddenly appeared. "I'm sorry, sir. I really am."

Mr. Foster turned to Virginia. "Thank you for speaking up." He called gruffly to Cory, "Mr. Blake, return to your seat. Miss Carter, you will clean up the glass. Then you will stay after class this afternoon and write in your copybook two hundred times, *I will not deceive the teacher.*"

"I c-can't stay after class today," Andi stammered. "My brother—"

"You *will* stay, Miss Carter. Is that understood?" When Andi nodded, he pointed to the remaining pieces of glass. "Fetch the broom and do as I ask, before I add a thrashing to your punishment."

The teacher's threat propelled Andi toward the back of the room like a cannon shot. When she passed Cory's desk, he handed her a hastily scribbled note. "Sorry," it read. "I was trying to make up for the snake."

Cramming the note into her dress pocket, Andi glanced at Cory. He gave her an apologetic smile. She forced a smile in return. Then she grabbed the broom and finished cleaning up the mess.

Chapter Six

A ROTTEN AFTERNOON

A ndi slammed her copybook shut and let out a weary sigh. For the past hour the only sound in the classroom had been the *scratch, scratch, scratch* of pen against paper as she scribbled out two hundred of the longest sentences of her life.

I will not deceive the teacher was burned into Andi's mind, but the hot flush that raced through her fingers as she wrote had nothing to do with shame or remorse over her behavior. Justin had promised to take her home right after school today. Now a whole hour of precious riding time was wasted. All because of—

"That spiteful Virginia Foster," Andi mumbled. She capped the ink jar, cleaned her pen tip, and placed the pen in her desk. "She waited until after her father whipped Cory to tell him who broke the window. She wanted to see both of us punished."

Andi glanced up quickly, hoping Mr. Foster hadn't heard her critical remark about his daughter. With a sigh of relief, she found the classroom deserted.

Why didn't you speak up sooner?

The accusation wormed its way into Andi's thoughts. She had no answer for her conscience, and it was too late now to go back and loosen her tongue. The damage was done.

Andi gathered her books and rose from her desk. She didn't know why the schoolmaster had stepped out, but she wasn't going to stick around and wait for his return. She'd already spent more time in town this afternoon than she liked.

The heat of her anger had dropped only a few degrees by the time she clattered down the stairs and burst through the double doors into the afternoon sun. Perhaps a brisk ride home would help her sort out her feelings. Maybe Justin would let her drive the buggy or—

Andi stopped short. Her brother stood next to the buggy, chatting with Mr. Foster. The sight of the men speaking together cooled Andi off faster than a bucket of cold water.

"Well, it's about time," Justin said when he saw her. He waved her over.

Andi pasted a smile on her face and joined them. "I'm finished, Mr. Foster," she forced herself to say. "May I go now?"

An unsmiling Mr. Foster nodded. "I hope this afternoon's copy work has been an exercise to help curb your exuberance," he said. "Has it?"

Andi wasn't sure what *exuberance* meant, but coming from the schoolmaster, she guessed it was not a compliment. "Yes, sir."

He shook his head and turned to Justin. "Perhaps you are unaware of this, Mr. Carter, but your sister is rather high-spirited." His tone oozed with disapproval. "And a touch reckless, I'm afraid."

"Really!" Justin raised his eyebrows. He looked like he was trying hard to keep a straight face.

"Yes indeed. However, with the proper guidance, it may be possible to bring her under control before it is too late."

"I'll give your remarks serious consideration," Justin said. "Now if you'll excuse us, it's a long drive back to the ranch."

"Of course. Good day." Mr. Foster shook Justin's hand, touched the brim of his hat to Andi, and turned to leave. "Tell your mother I'm looking forward to Saturday," were his parting words.

Andi stared at Mr. Foster's retreating form. Reckless? High-spirited? Out of control? How could he say such—

"Do you plan on standing here all afternoon, or would you like a ride home?" Justin reached out a helping hand.

Andi grasped his hand and swung herself into the rig. She pushed Mr. Foster's unkind words into a corner of her mind. "Where's Rosa?"

Justin climbed up beside her. "She got tired of waiting and caught a ride back to the ranch with her father. He was in town picking up supplies for Chad."

"I suppose you got tired of waiting too."

"Yes, I did." Justin chirruped to the horse, and they started down the street. "That's why I came looking for you."

"Did Rosa tell you what happened?"

"No, but Mr. Foster did."

Silence.

Justin flicked the reins across Pal's back. "May I look at the sentences?"

Andi felt a warm flush creep into her cheeks. She pulled out her copybook and opened it to four pages of small, neat script.

Justin took the book with his free hand and skimmed the lines. "Would you care to explain to me why you lied to your teacher?"

No, I wouldn't care to explain, Andi wanted to say. But she took a deep breath and plunged into the whole awful story. It didn't take long to tell.

"That's pretty much the same story I heard from Mr. Foster." Justin closed the copybook and dropped it in her lap. "However, his retelling was sprinkled with several unflattering comments about your behavior in his classroom."

"I didn't mean to deceive him, Justin. I tried to tell him, but I was so scared. The words got stuck. Then Cory jumped in and . . . well, you know the rest."

"I know you got yourself into another fix by not speaking up when you should have. Mr. Foster is strict, but I think his punishment was fair. We'll work out a way you can pay for the window, and that will be the end of it."

"It *won't* be the end of it! Mr. Foster's always riding me for anything he thinks might be the least bit improper for a young lady." She grimaced. "And your being on the school board doesn't help."

"Actually, I think your troubles began just before school started. Nearly trampling your teacher wasn't the best way to begin the term, but I'm sure Mr. Foster will eventually put it behind him. After all, he did drop the malicious mischief charges."

"Only because I'm your sister."

Justin chuckled. "See? I'm good for something." He pulled Andi into a hug. "Once Mr. Foster becomes comfortable with his pupils, and the older boys figure out who's in charge, I think he'll turn out to be a good schoolmaster. Just do me a favor and try to stay out of trouble. And be patient."

Be patient? Patience was not one of her strong points. Andi realized Justin knew that too. That's why he was smiling.

"I'll try, Justin. I really will," she promised.

"Good." He slapped the reins, and the large bay horse, which had slowed to a lazy walk during the conversation, broke into a trot.

Andi rode in silence for a few miles. She mourned the fact that everything was going wrong on what should have been a perfect afternoon. The late summer sun had turned from scorching hot to pleasantly warm the past few days—perfect for a good, fast ride on her horse. Her mother had promised Andi that she would have time to ride if she came right home.

She scowled. Most of her free time today had been taken up writing sentences. When she arrived home, she'd have to tell Mother about the broken window. When she did, Andi would most likely find herself with half a dozen unpleasant chores to pay for it. Worse, her favorite brother—while not exactly angry— didn't seem sympathetic to her problems. Worst of all, Virginia Foster was—

"Justin!" Andi jerked up from where she had been slouched against the seat, idly watching the scenery go by.

"What is it?" Justin asked, turning the buggy onto the wide lane that led up to the ranch house.

"Remember back in town? You were talking with Mr. Foster about Saturday." She took a deep breath. "What's happening on Saturday?"

"We're having the new schoolmaster and his family out to the ranch for supper. A welcoming meal and some friendly conversation."

Andi stared at her brother in disbelief. "The entire family? Virginia too?"

"Of course."

"This is terrible! Mother will expect me to entertain Virginia."

"Probably. Why shouldn't you entertain her for an afternoon?"

"Because whenever I'm with Virginia, something dreadful happens. You don't know her like I do."

Justin slowed the horse to a walk. "You can't know her very well. School has been in session barely two weeks."

"I've known her long enough to figure out that we're never going to be friends. She's sneaky and mean and . . ." Andi slumped against the seat. This conversation was not going well. "And she can't take a joke. She blamed *me* for Cory's snake being in her desk, even though it wasn't my fault. She thinks I'm some kind of rowdy tomboy."

"She probably also holds it against you for nearly killing her father," Justin added.

"That too," Andi agreed with a heavy heart. "So you see, I simply *cannot* entertain Virginia on Saturday. She doesn't like me at all." She gave her brother a pleading look. "You understand, don't you?"

"Of course. I understand perfectly." Justin eyed her. "But I doubt Mother will."

Andi groaned. Justin was right, as usual. Mother would not understand. Even if she did sympathize, it wouldn't make the slightest difference. Mother would expect Andi to set aside her own feelings and entertain Virginia Foster for as long as the family stayed. Showing hospitality—whether one liked the guests or even knew them—was an unspoken rule on the Circle C ranch.

"Will you talk to Mother for me? This once?"

"Sorry, honey," Justin said. "I'm afraid this is one area over which I have no influence. Even Father bowed to Mother's wishes when it came to entertaining guests. If you knew how often Chad and I got our backsides tanned for misbehaving when unwelcome guests came calling . . ." A smile pulled at the corners of his mouth.

"Tell me!"

"The time I remember best was when Chad stuffed Freddy Stone's foul mouth full of dirt and tossed him into the horse trough."

Andi laughed.

"It wasn't funny at the time," Justin said. "Freddy was one of those annoying little boys who dressed like a sissy and behaved perfectly around the adults, but he played dirty tricks on the other kids. Chad decided a whipping was a fair price to pay for entertaining Freddy in a way he'd never forget."

"I bet it was something," Andi remarked in delight. Perhaps she was talking to the wrong brother. Maybe Chad would sympathize enough to offer her a workable solution.

"I'm sure things will go fine on Saturday," Justin said, "so long as you're not tempted to toss Virginia into the horse trough."

"That's not funny, big brother."

Justin was still chuckling when they drove through the gate and into the yard. He pulled the horse to a stop and gave an appreciative whistle. "Take a look at that." A magnificent dappled-gray horse pranced around the corral about a dozen yards away.

Andi gasped. "They got him, Justin! They finally caught Whirlwind." She nearly fell from the buggy in her hurry to see the horse. As soon as her feet touched the ground, she took off running toward the corral.

She had gone six steps when a pair of strong hands grabbed her waist and swung her around. "Whoa there, little sister." Chad's voice carried a hint of warning. "Where do you think you're headed?"

"Oh, Chad! You got him. Can't I see him up close?" She tried to wriggle free from her brother's grasp, but he held on tight and shook his head.

"Not yet. He's too spooked. It'll be awhile before anyone goes near him. I want you, especially, to stay away from him. Do you hear me?"

"But—"

"No, Andi."

Andi settled down and watched the beautiful horse run around the corral. She'd almost lost her life last spring because of her disobedience in going near one of her brother's wild stallions. Perhaps Chad knew best, after all.

"He's a beauty." She turned around. "Where did you catch him?"

"Up in the hills." Chad looked mighty pleased with himself. He crossed his arms and watched the horse with satisfaction. "It took a couple of weeks, but we finally caught up with him and his band this morning. Got the mares back too."

"What're you going to do with him?"

"Break him, I hope. Then sell him. He's good horseflesh, even with that wild streak." He grinned. "You want to help?"

Andi looked up into her brother's bright-blue eyes and gasped. Was he teasing her? "Me? You mean it?"

"I sure do," he said. "Give me a couple of weeks with him first. I'll be able to judge him better after that. If it looks like he's going to behave himself, I'll let you help with some of the gentling. I can't promise more than that, and I don't know what Mother will say to any of it."

Andi threw her arms around Chad's waist and gave him a grateful hug. "You don't have to worry about what Mother will say. She always lets you make the ranch decisions." She grinned. "You're the ranch boss."

"I sure am. Make sure you don't forget it," Chad warned her. "Stay away from that horse. Right now he's dangerous. Don't let your curiosity get the better of you."

"I won't. I'll do anything you say."

"Good. How about starting on your chores?"

Andi's joy vanished. "Oh. Yeah. Chores." She made no move to begin.

Chad took her by the shoulders and spun her around in the direction of the horse barn. "The chores are that way. Feed the horses and make sure you check their water. It's been pretty hot lately. When you're finished, you can straighten up your tack. You've got bridles and brushes and your saddle and blanket scattered from one end of the barn to the other. We have a tack room, you know."

"I know." Andi shrugged away from her brother's hold, crossed the yard, and entered the barn. "Taffy! I'm home." She glanced around the dim interior, hoping Mitch might be nearby. Twice last week he'd helped her with her chores. Maybe he would do them again today so she could ride Taffy longer.

Andi heard a scraping sound and spun around. A large shadow filled the doorway, blocking the afternoon sun. She grinned, all set to charm Mitch into giving her some help. Her smile faded when she recognized Chad leaning against the doorpost.

"Expecting somebody else?" His lips twitched. Before Andi could reply, he continued, "If you think you can sweet-talk Mitch into doing your chores again today, it's too late. I sent him on a cattle-buying trip. He won't be home 'til Friday."

Andi snatched up a hoof pick and hurled it at her brother. She was furious that he could so easily figure out what she was thinking. Chad caught the pick and dropped it into a grooming box. Then he turned and left the barn, laughing softly.

Andi ripped apart the dry, sweet-smelling alfalfa hay and began pitching it to the hungry horses in their stalls. When she reached Taffy's stall, she paused. "I tell you, Taffy, I've had one miserable day. What do you say I finish up here in a hurry, change clothes, and then we go for a ride?"

Taffy snorted her agreement and tossed her head.

Andi gave the mare a friendly pat and whispered, "*Then* I'll tell Mother about the broken window."

Chapter Seven

CIRCLE C HOSPITALITY

A ndi lay across her sister's bed in gloomy silence and watched seventeen-year-old Melinda brush out her golden hair. She arranged it in a complicated style and turned away from the mirror. Her hands held up heavy lengths of blond ringlets. "So," she mumbled through lips crammed full of hairpins, "what do you think?"

"Hmmm." Andi cocked her head and regarded her sister carefully. "I don't think you'll be able to eat very well, not with your hands holding your hair up like that."

Melinda's expression twisted in annoyance. She opened her mouth, and the hairpins fell to the floor. "Andrea Carter, you know good and well what I meant." She dropped her hands to her sides with an exasperated sigh. Her hair tumbled past her shoulders in disarray.

Andi sat up. "I don't know why you're fixing your hair and dressing so fancy. You won't be able to take a decent breath after you lace your corset up tight." She shuddered at the thought of sacrificing comfort for fashion. "It's only the Fosters coming for supper—not Jeffrey Sullivan."

Melinda began collecting hairpins from the floor. "Just because we live on a ranch doesn't mean we can't look and act like ladies. The Fosters are newly arrived from back East. Do you know what that means?"

Andi grinned. "That they're greenhorns?"

"No, silly!" Melinda rolled her eyes. "It means Grace is acquainted with all the latest hairstyles and fashions. She's bringing her most recent copies of *Godey's Lady's Book* to go through. I want to look nice for our guests."

An idea popped into Andi's head. She dropped to the floor, scooped up the rest of the hairpins, and handed them over with a smile. "Melinda, I think your hair looks beautiful, like always. You're the nicest, prettiest sister in the whole world." She paused.

"What are you up to?" Melinda asked.

"Nothing. It's just . . . well, Virginia would love to look at fashion plates and talk about the latest Eastern styles too, I bet. Why don't you invite her to join you?"

"Sorry, Andi, but Grace and I have already made our plans." Melinda returned to her seat, picked up a brush, and began vigorously attacking her hair.

Andi plopped back onto the bed. "Aw, c'mon. If you entertain Virginia along with her sister, I'll do whatever you ask for a whole week. I'll make your bed, clean your room, brush your horse . . ."

She took a deep breath. "I'll even be nice to Jeffrey Sullivan when he comes calling tomorrow after church. Please, Melinda. I *can't* spend an afternoon with Virginia."

Her sister was her last hope. She'd gotten nowhere with her brothers.

Melinda jabbed a hairpin into a stubborn lock of gold. "Honestly, Andi, she can't be as bad as you say. Grace is delightful."

"Virginia is not."

"Why don't you show Virginia your horse?" Melinda suggested. "Maybe you and she can go riding."

"Ha!" Andi scoffed. "She probably doesn't know which end of the horse to bridle."

"Andi!" Melinda's eyes opened wide. "That was unkind."

"I'm sorry, but you don't know what she's like. She acts perfect and ladylike in front of her father, but she's a different person when he's not around. And she's always showing off how smart she is."

"You better not let Mother hear you talk that way," Melinda warned. "Virginia's our guest, and it's your responsibility to amuse her this afternoon."

"So everyone keeps telling me," Andi said. "How am I supposed to do that?"

"By conducting yourself like a Christian young lady and remembering your duty as a hostess," a new voice broke in. Smiling, Mother glided into the bedroom. "I realize Virginia and you might not have much in common, Andrea. I'm not asking you to make her your best friend. Just treat her with courtesy and kindness. Remember? Do unto others . . ." She paused.

"As I would have others do unto me," Andi finished.

She'd heard the Golden Rule plenty of times before, and she usually tried to remember it. But with Virginia? "Can't I stay in my room this afternoon? You could tell the Fosters I'm ill." She laid a hand over her stomach and winced. "I really don't feel very well."

Mother joined Andi on the bed. "You can't hide from people you don't like, sweetheart. Part of growing up is learning to get along with folks, especially those who rub you the wrong way. I'm sure if you look beyond Virginia's shortcomings, you'll find something pleasant to talk about."

"Like what?"

"I heard the Fosters visited Yosemite a few weeks ago. You could encourage her to talk about her trip. Or you could ask her how she likes it out West. Perhaps if you show an interest in some of the things she's seen or done, she'll warm up."

Andi sighed. "Mother, she thinks I'm a tomboy. She doesn't want anything to do with me." *And I don't want anything to do with her*, she added silently.

"You might show her another side," Mother suggested. "The polite and well-mannered daughter I've raised. Show a little compassion to a newcomer, Andrea. Virginia has been uprooted, moved from everything familiar, and set down in the middle of a small, dusty town. She's probably frightened and insecure, unsure how to act around the other girls."

Mother smiled. "Do you remember a few years ago when I took over your classroom because Miss Hall had an accident?"

Andi nodded. She would never forget those few weeks.

"At first, you didn't like the idea of your mother teaching class, did you?"

"No," Andi admitted.

"Now put yourself in Virginia's place. Her father is the schoolmaster. From what Justin tells me, the man has high standards for both academics and behavior. Imagine having to live up to those kinds of expectations."

Mother's words turned Andi's thoughts upside down. She had firsthand experience with Mr. Foster's strict demands. She couldn't imagine the man as her father. A twinge of compassion for Virginia stirred in Andi's heart.

Mother rose from the bed. "In spite of the way you feel about each other, I know you will extend to Virginia a full measure of Circle C hospitality."

It was not a request.

"I'll do my best, Mother," Andi said. "But it won't be easy."

"I didn't say it would be easy. Perhaps a quick prayer while you're changing clothes will help keep you in the right frame of mind. Now, run along. It's nearly time for our guests to arrive."

"Yes, ma'am." Andi trudged to her room, peeled off her Saturday overalls, and slipped a pale-green frock over her head. She ran a brush through the tangles of unruly dark waves that fell to her waist and then braided her hair in a hurry.

"This is going to be a long afternoon," she whispered to her reflection in the vanity mirror. Then she raised her gaze to the ceiling. "I

59

really want to get along with Virginia, Lord. No matter how much she riles me today, please help me keep my temper."

Andi left her room in better spirits and headed for the stairs, where she met Rosa. "I sure wish I was dusting the second floor today and *you* were amusing Virginia."

Rosa's cloth swirled along the banister railing. "Days like these make me glad that I am the hired girl. I would not trade places with you for all the gold in California."

Andi didn't blame her. She eyed the railing, weighed the consequences of sliding in her Sunday frock, and wisely chose to walk down the stairs.

The afternoon started off pleasantly enough. There were polite greetings all around. Melinda and Grace headed for the library, where they could talk and giggle in private.

Andi greeted Virginia and offered to show her around. "Would you like to see my room? It has a balcony and—"

"No." Virginia brushed aside a pale wisp of hair and smoothed down her skirt. "I don't want to stay indoors. I want to see the ranch."

Andi threw her a suspicious look.

"That is not a good idea, darling," Mrs. Foster said. "You're not used to the climate yet. It's unbearably hot outside, and the dust will soil your new frock. You should stay indoors with the others." She looked at her hostess. "Later, Virginia has a musical piece to share. She plays piano so well."

"That will be lovely," Mother agreed.

"Do you play the piano, Andrea?" Mrs. Foster asked.

"No, ma'am. But I ride pretty well."

It was the wrong thing to say, Andi realized in a flash. Any mention of horseback riding was sure to bring back dreadful memories for the Fosters.

"Perhaps Virginia would like to practice her piece," Mother suggested smoothly. "Andrea would be happy to listen."

Andi straightened up at her mother's intense gaze. "I sure would. Come on, Virginia. I'll show you the—"

"No." Virginia's dark eyes filled with tears. "I don't want to practice my piece. I want to go outdoors. Please, Mama. You never let me do anything. I want to see the ranch."

"But, darling," Mrs. Foster tried again, "it's dangerous."

Virginia stood firm.

"The Circle C is no more dangerous than the streets of Fresno," Mother assured her. "In some ways, it's safer. Andrea will make sure Virginia comes to no harm. She knows the ranch well."

"All right then," Mrs. Foster conceded with a sigh. "But keep your sunbonnet on, darling. Your skin cannot take this harsh western sun."

"Yes, Mama." Virginia pulled the strings to her bonnet forward. "Come on, Andrea. Let's go."

Andi didn't move. This was a terrible idea. She did not want to be responsible for Virginia's safety. "I think Mrs. Foster is right, Mother. Maybe we'd better stay inside."

It was no use. Mother handed Andi her hat. "Have a lovely time, girls." She opened the door.

Andi plopped her black felt hat onto her head and followed Virginia out of the house.

Once they were alone, Virginia giggled. "You look silly wearing that old hat with your party dress."

"It keeps the sun off, same as your bonnet. Now, what do you want to see?"

Virginia rolled her eyes. "I only wanted to go outdoors to get away. Mama hovers over me all the time." She sighed. "Mothers can be such a trial, don't you agree?"

Andi did *not* agree, but it wouldn't do any good to say it aloud. "Would you like to go riding?" she asked. If Virginia agreed, perhaps the afternoon wouldn't be a complete waste.

Virginia's eyes lit up. Then she shook her head and smoothed down her skirt. "Heavens, no! I'd soil my dress. If I'd known you wanted to ride, I would have worn my habit."

Andi looked at Virginia in surprise. She actually knew how to ride? "Well, maybe another time you and I could—"

"Oh my goodness! What a magnificent animal!" Virginia pointed toward the corral. Chad's rogue stallion paced back and forth along the inside of the fence. His mane and tail shimmered. "What's his name?"

Andi's spirits soared. Virginia liked horses? Perhaps this was the "something pleasant" Mother suggested they could talk about. "His name's Whirlwind. Isn't he a beauty? Chad's breaking him, and"— she grinned—"he's letting me help."

Virginia gasped. "Why would he let you do that? Isn't he afraid you'll be hurt? That horse looks so . . . so wild."

"He is." Andi smiled wider. "Chad knows what he's doing."

Virginia watched Whirlwind circle the corral. Her face showed her longing. "When will he be ready to ride?"

"Not for a long, long time."

"My father promised Gracie and me a horse if we moved out West," Virginia said. "Perhaps I'll tell him we want this one."

Andi laughed. "Are you crazy? You can't ride Whirlwind." She wasn't even sure Chad would let *her* ride him.

Virginia narrowed her eyes. "How dare you laugh! Do you think I can't ride a horse?"

Andi didn't know *what* to think. "Even after Chad breaks him, Whirlwind is not the saddle horse for you or your sister. He's too spirited. If your father wants to buy you a horse, though, we have some nice—"

"Oh, and you think you know which horse is good for us?" Virginia jammed her hands on her hips and glared at Andi.

"I didn't mean to make you angry," Andi said. "I only meant—"

"I think I'd like to go riding after all," Virginia snapped. She lifted her skirts and hurried toward the horse barn.

Andi scurried to catch up. "We have to go inside and change first." Virginia stopped. "Whatever for?"

"You told me you didn't want to spoil your dress. I have riding clothes you can borrow."

A shadow fell across Virginia's face. "If I go in the house, Mama will insist I rest or read or practice my piece." She shook her head. "I'm . . . I'm going riding."

Andi heard the hesitation in Virginia's voice. "You *can* ride, can't you?"

"Of course I can." Virginia flounced her skirts and headed for the barn.

Andi followed Virginia inside, where she soon discovered she had two horses to tack up. Virginia didn't lift a finger to help. She acted hurt when Andi suggested it. "I don't want to soil my dress," she gave as her excuse.

Andi bit her tongue to keep from reminding her guest how dirty she would get from riding. Did she think saddles were boiled to keep them clean? Or that the dust would stay where Virginia commanded it?

By the time Andi finished getting Taffy and Pal ready, she was sweating. Hauling around two saddles was twice the work. She shoved a set of reins into Virginia's hands. "Let's go."

Once outside, Virginia patted Pal in all the wrong places, circled him twice, and examined each part of the bridle and saddle with exasperating care.

"Are you going to mount up anytime soon?" Andi leaned against Taffy and crossed her arms over her chest. "It's not hard. You put your left foot in the stirrup, grab the saddle horn, and hike yourself up. Like this."

Andi tucked her foot in the stirrup and swung up into the saddle. She patted Taffy's neck and then jumped back down and brushed off her skirt. "That's all there is to it."

Virginia pouted. "You act like you don't believe I can ride."

"Can you?"

"I said I could!" She reached hesitant fingers toward the stirrup and slipped her foot into place. Shooting an annoyed look at Andi, Virginia curled her hands around the saddle horn. Then she took a deep breath and eased herself off the ground.

Pal shied away.

Virginia shrieked and nearly lost her footing. Andi lent a helping hand to her guest's backside and boosted her into the saddle.

"Virginia . . ." A wave of uneasiness washed over Andi when she saw how tightly Virginia was clutching the saddle horn. What if she was all talk? What if she couldn't ride after all? What if—

"I'm going to mount up behind you," Andi decided. "We can ride double for a while."

"Nonsense! I'll show *you*, Andrea Carter, that it's no great trick to ride a horse." She raised her heels in the air.

"No, Virginia! Don't kick him!" Andi lunged for the bridle.

Too late.

Virginia jammed her heels into Pal's flank. The startled horse snorted his surprise and took off at a full gallop across the yard.

Chapter Eight

AN ENCOUNTER WITH A
WHIRLWIND

A ndi didn't waste a second. She leaped onto Taffy and started after her blundering guest. "Pull back on the reins!" she yelled, before realizing Virginia didn't have the reins. They were flapping wildly around Pal's neck and head.

Virginia shrieked—and kept on shrieking.

Andi raced to catch up. Poor Pal was trying to run away from the noisy nuisance on his back. "Hang on!" Andi shouted. "And stop yelling!"

Virginia was screaming too loudly to hear. Then suddenly, miraculously, one of the reins flew up to where Virginia could snatch it. She yanked.

Pal turned abruptly and raced back toward the corrals and outbuildings. Horse and rider hurtled past Andi. She pulled Taffy around and continued the chase. Grudging admiration and relief swept through her. It appeared that Virginia was not about to get herself dumped.

Andi's relief was short-lived. Whirlwind's corral loomed in front of the riders. The wild horse pranced and whinnied, clearly agitated at the screams, and at seeing the other horses running around the yard.

Pal rushed headlong toward the corral, guided by Virginia's one-handed grip on the reins. Andi watched in horror, helpless to do anything to stop it.

Then it was over. Pal came to a bone-jarring stop at the corral fence. Wailing, Virginia flew over the fence and crumpled to the ground with a dull thud. Her cries ceased instantly.

"Virginia!" Andi caught her breath in horror. She slid from Taffy's back and rushed to the corral. "Say something! Are you all right?"

There was no answer.

Andi squeezed between the railings, heedless of the ripping sound when her skirt caught and tore. She threw herself down beside Virginia and shook her. "Wake up, Virginia," she pleaded. *Oh God, please let her be all right!*

A sudden flash of dappled gray thundered past the girls. Andi looked up just as Whirlwind took a mighty leap and sailed effortlessly over the corral fence. He kicked up his hooves and made a mad dash for freedom, leaving a billowing cloud of dust behind.

"Oh no!" Andi slumped. "Chad's gonna skin me alive."

Whimpering sounds drew Andi's attention back to her guest. A trembling Virginia sat up and looked around. "Where am I?" Then her eyes widened in memory. "Oh! That wild beast of a horse! He threw me."

Pal stood quietly on the other side of the fence. He rubbed his nose against a post and flicked his tail.

"Pal's not wild. He stopped, and you kept going." Andi was too drained to feel anything but relief that Virginia was not seriously hurt. "You lied about being able to ride, didn't you?"

"You put me on a wild horse, to make it appear that I couldn't ride," Virginia accused. Then she noticed her clothes. "Look at my dress. It's so full of dirt it will never come clean."

Andi frowned and rose to her feet. She offered Virginia her hand. "Never mind about your silly dress. Just be thankful you're alive. Now, let's get out of here."

Virginia grasped Andi's hand and struggled to stand. "Ooh! My head hurts." She took a step and stumbled. Andi gripped her arm and kept her upright.

A shout drew Andi's attention to the house. A ranch hand galloped up. He dismounted and banged on the main door. "Boss! We got trouble." The door opened, and he disappeared inside.

A moment later, the door flew open. Andi's three brothers raced toward the corral. The rest of the family and their guests hurried after them. They stopped short at the sight of the two girls standing in the empty corral.

Chad, as usual, reacted first. "I don't believe it!" He slammed his palm against the corral post and glared at his sister. "Get yourself out of there—right now."

Andi jumped to obey. She yanked on Virginia's hand and hurried out of the enclosure.

Virginia broke into a loud wail and fell into her mother's arms. "Oh, Mama, I've never been so frightened in my life. I could have been killed."

Mr. Foster joined his wife and daughter. "What happened here, daughter? What were you doing in that filthy pen?"

Virginia buried her head against her mother and cried louder.

"We were riding," Andi said. "Pal got away from—"

"Riding!" Mr. Foster's face paled. "Virginia doesn't ride."

Andi's heart dropped to her toes. *I should have known.* "B-but she said—"

"She tricked me into riding a wild beast of a horse," Virginia sobbed. "I didn't want to, but she promised it wouldn't hurt me. I told her I can't ride, but she boosted me into the saddle and slapped that nasty horse on the rump."

Mrs. Foster gasped.

"He ran away with me and threw me, and . . . and . . ." Virginia gulped. "Take me home, Mama."

"Virginia!" Andi cried out. "How can you tell such dreadful lies?"

Mrs. Foster turned to Mother. "Mrs. Carter, I scarcely know what to say. My husband was nearly run over by these brutish western horses, and now my daughter has a similar experience." She gave Pal a fierce look. "It's a miracle Virginia didn't break her neck."

"It's her own fault." Andi clenched her fists. "She told me she—"

"Andrea." Mother warned with a frown. Then she turned to the Fosters. "Let's settle Virginia in the parlor with a cool drink. I'm certain she will feel much better by the time supper is served."

"I'm afraid we must decline your offer, Mrs. Carter," Mr. Foster said. "I would like to take Virginia home. Besides, I fear I've lost my appetite." He motioned to his wife and daughters. "Come, Margaret, Grace. We're leaving."

With a stiff good-bye, the Foster family made their way to their large black surrey. Mr. Foster settled his family and turned for a final word. "I do not mean to sound presumptuous, ma'am, but let me suggest that what your wild girl needs is a serious thrashing. Perhaps that might curb her independent and reckless spirit." He took his place on the seat, flicked the reins, and drove away.

Andi bit her tongue to keep from crying out at Mr. Foster's cruel words. Blinking back tears of rage and shame, she watched the surrey disappear down the road. She knew she should try to explain this disaster to her mother, but her throat tightened up.

Nobody spoke. It was as if an enormous black cloud had suddenly settled over the ranch, dampening everyone's mood. Andi knew Chad, especially, must be sore. The time and effort he'd spent in capturing Whirlwind had just gone to waste, all because of one lying girl. "I'm sorry the stallion got out, Chad," she said, "but—"

"I trusted you, Andi," Chad stormed. "I thought we had an agreement." He threw up his hands. "It took us two weeks to capture that animal. He'll waste no time rounding up those mares again, and we'll be right back where we started. Not to mention how *dangerous*—"

"It wasn't my fault!" Andi yelled. "I didn't go near him. Honest, I didn't. Whirlwind got spooked when Virginia landed in the corral."

"I don't care whose fault it is. You were in the corral. Now the horse is gone."

"Is this really necessary?" their mother broke in. "Granted, the stallion's escape is an annoyance, but the important thing is that no one was injured. Shouting at each other will not bring back that horse."

Chad sighed. "You're right, Mother. I'll round up some of the men and see if we can track the stallion down." He gave Andi a disgusted look, then turned on his heel and headed for the bunkhouse.

"Now, Andrea," Mother said when Chad was out of sight. "What really happened?"

Andi took a deep breath. "Virginia lied about knowing how to ride. Pal took off with her. I was so scared. I went after her on Taffy, but it was too late. She didn't know how to control him. When Pal stopped, Virginia went head over heels into the corral. Before I knew what was happening, Whirlwind raced past us and jumped the fence."

She gave her mother a tiny smile. "You should've seen him, Mother. He was beautiful, flying over that fence."

Then Andi lost her smile. Whirlwind was gone. Even if Chad managed to capture him again, she doubted he'd let her have anything to do with gentling him. Not now. Not after this disaster.

Mother put an arm around her. "I believe you, sweetheart, and I'm sorry Mr. Foster spoke as he did. He must have been very frightened when he learned what happened." She gave Andi a hug. "It's a mercy that Virginia escaped with no more than a good scare and a few bruises. Losing the stallion pales next to what could have happened."

"Yes, ma'am," Andi whispered. She was thankful Virginia was still in one piece. But still . . . "What about Chad? He's awful sore at me."

Justin glanced toward the bunkhouse. "Soon as he gets the stallion back, Chad will simmer down. But if you like, I'll go talk to him."

"Oh yes. Please do." Justin always knew what to say.

Mitch gave one of Andi's braids an affectionate tug. "Think I'll give Chad a hand with that stallion. It'll give him somebody else to yell at for a while." He headed after Justin.

Melinda grasped Andi's hand and squeezed. "I'll take care of Taffy and Pal. You go along with Mother and wash up."

Andi smiled at her sister. "Thanks, Melinda."

Heading back to the house, Andi realized the afternoon had gone exactly as she'd warned Justin it would, but it gave her no satisfaction to know she'd been right. Virginia had disrupted Andi's life. She was the cause of a quarrel between Andi and her brother. She had proved to be the biggest liar west of the Sierras and yet had managed to wheedle her way out of any blame.

Instead of being scolded for her lie, Virginia had been comforted with soft words. Worst of all, Mr. Foster had called Andi wild and reckless. Perhaps it was true—a little—but that wasn't the cause of today's disaster.

Andi washed up until the water in the bowl turned dark. Then she threw herself on her bed and buried her head in her pillow. *Oh Lord,* she prayed, *I can't get along with Virginia, and I don't even want to try anymore. She's mean and spiteful. Surely You don't expect me to forgive her for this? I can't!*

She was still stewing when a quiet knock sounded at her door, and her mother called her to supper.

Chapter Nine

ANDI LOSES HER TEMPER

Q*ué te pasa?*"
Andi looked up from where she sat on the front steps of the schoolhouse. Rosa was watching her with concern. "Nothing's the matter with me. I just want to sit here." She went back to watching the students run around the schoolyard. "You're not supposed to be speaking Spanish," she reminded her friend.

Rosa smiled. "No one can hear me but you." She settled herself next to Andi, opened her lunch pail, and took out a cold tamale. "Do you want this? It's your favorite. You know my mother makes the best tamales in the valley."

A smile replaced Andi's frown, but she shook her head. "I'm not hungry."

"You should forget about Saturday," Rosa advised. She unwrapped the meat-filled tamale from its cornhusk covering and took a bite. "*Señor* Chad got his horse back, *no?*" she asked between mouthfuls.

Andi nodded. "Last night."

"Now your brother is no longer angry, right?"

"Wrong. Justin tried to smooth things over, but Chad's tired and grouchy. He didn't say more than two words to me all weekend." She drew a deep breath. "I know Luisa's upset, and your mother is too, seeing that their special company dinner was only picked at. Nobody felt much like eating."

"I ate it," Rosa said cheerfully. "So did *Papá* and Joselito. *Mamá* also gave some to the ranch hands." She forced part of the tamale into Andi's hand. "Here. Eat." She unwrapped another tamale and continued. "What did the *señora* say about all this?"

Andi took a bite of the tamale. "We had a long talk Saturday evening. Actually, Mother did most of the talking. I was too busy bawling. She said I had to learn to get along with Virginia, no matter how I felt, and that meant forgiving her for lying."

"*¡Ay, no!*" Rosa grimaced.

"After what Virginia did, I don't want to forgive her or even look at her. And I've lost any chance of ever getting Mr. Foster to like me." She slumped. "Did you notice I got another failing mark in geography this morning?"

Rosa started on another tamale. "I noticed."

Andi finished her tamale then propped her elbows on her knees and rested her chin in her hands. "That's the second time I've gotten low marks this term. Mother's not going to like it. Mr. Foster expects each of us to know all the answers when we recite. I can't remember all those silly facts about rivers, mountains, exports, and imports in South America."

"Virginia knows all the answers," Rosa said.

Andi rolled her eyes. "Virginia's at the top of every class, from arithmetic to spelling. She's so smart that she makes the rest of us look like dunces. I don't know if she's a good student because she enjoys learning or because she likes to show off." She paused in thought. "Or maybe she's afraid of failing because her father's the schoolmaster."

Andi could understand that feeling. "A couple of years ago, when Miss Hall sprained her ankle, the school board asked Mother to teach our class. I didn't want to go to school. I was afraid the kids would laugh. Johnny Wilson tried to get me in trouble—just to find out if Mother would punish her own child. I thought I had to do everything perfectly, or Mother would be shamed."

"You think Virginia feels the same about her father?"

"I don't know. Maybe. I've heard some of the kids call her 'teacher's pet.' I also know she's a different person when Mr. Foster's not around." Andi sighed. "I'd feel sorry for her and try harder to be a friend if she hadn't lied and gotten me into so much trouble with Chad."

"She does not want to be your friend," Rosa said.

Andi accepted another tamale. "I know, but my mother thinks Virginia is lonely and unhappy. She wants me to try to be friends with her. You know, the Golden Rule and all that."

Rosa wrinkled her brow. "*¿Cómo?*"

In quick, forbidden Spanish, Andi explained the meaning of the English words.

"The *señora* is wise," Rosa said.

"Actually, my mother didn't think of it. She got it from the Bible. They're Jesus's words. 'As ye would that men should do to you, do ye also to them likewise,'" she quoted.

Rosa nodded her approval.

"Hey, Andi!" A breathless Cory Blake raced up. "Come play ball. The teams are uneven. We need you." He grabbed Andi's hand. Her tamale went flying.

Andi shook herself loose from his grasp. "Are you crazy? I don't want to play." She hadn't played ball since she'd broken the window the week before.

"You've been moping around all morning," Cory said. "All on account of what happened with that lying Virginia Foster. A good, fast ball game is just what you need to make you forget about her."

Rosa laughed. "He is right, *amiga*. You are happy when you run and play ball."

Playing ball was not a good idea. "I shouldn't have told you a thing."

"I would've found out." Cory laughed. "Come on."

"Oh, all right." Andi jumped up and brushed off the back of her skirt. She flicked a quick glance toward the half-open doorway at the top of the steps, just to make sure Mr. Foster wasn't spying on her. He wasn't.

But Virginia apparently was. She stood, half-hidden in the shadows behind the door. Her face peeked out through the opening, and her fingers gripped the edge of the door. Two spots of pink colored her pale cheeks.

"I heard you, Andrea Carter," she burst out, throwing open the door. "I heard you and your friends talking about me. You're mean and thoughtless. But it's nothing I didn't expect from this horde of uncultured, backward Westerners."

Heat rose to Andi's cheeks. She couldn't remember all she'd said to Rosa, but Cory's "that lying Virginia Foster" echoed fresh in her mind. What would Mother say if she knew about their unkindness? And after explaining the Golden Rule to Rosa too!

Andi opened her mouth to apologize, but what came out was, "Why did you lie about the accident being my fault?"

"I didn't," Virginia said. "You should have warned me about that horse."

"You should have told me you can't ride."

"I *can* ride," Virginia insisted. "But not a wild, half-broke horse."

Andi laughed at Virginia's outrageous claim. Half-broke horse? Ridiculous! It wasn't Pal's fault his rider was a ninny. "Anybody with a lick of sense and the teeniest bit of horsemanship can ride Pal. You couldn't, and he knew it."

She suddenly didn't feel like apologizing. Instead, the ball game sounded better and better. She clattered down the remaining steps. "Come on, Cory. Let's go."

Just as Cory and Rosa promised, Andi's drooping spirits soared. It wasn't long before she was so caught up in the ball game that she forgot everything else. She would not have cared if Mr. Foster himself were standing on the sidelines. Another two hundred sentences was worth getting her mind off Virginia.

The noon hour flew by. With only five minutes remaining, Cory's team lagged behind by only one run. He handed Andi the bat and gave her a serious look. "This is it, Andi. You're up. Davy's on base. There are two outs. Hit him in and we tie. Hit a home run and we win. Hit a window and we're dead. Can you do it?"

Andi brushed aside a sweaty lock of hair, looked at the pitcher, and grinned. "Sure I can." She gripped the bat and swung it up to her shoulder.

Cory returned her grin. "Good luck."

Andi knew it was a good pitch the instant the ball left Johnny's hand. She smacked the ball, tossed the bat aside, and took off running for first base. She crossed first and second to shouts of encouragement. She was past third base and on her way home when she heard Cory's frantic shout. "You gotta slide, Andi!"

Slide? Was the ball really that close?

Andi didn't look for herself. She did what her teammate told her and slid for home plate, sending up a rolling cloud of dust. Her feet touched the plate just seconds before the catcher snagged the ball.

"Safe! We won!" Cory yanked Andi to her feet and pounded her on the back. Dust flew everywhere.

Davy shook her hand. "Good hit."

Andi beamed.

"You were just lucky," Johnny muttered.

Andi scowled at Johnny, nodded her thanks to the others, and began slapping the dirt from her skirt. She sneezed.

A loud clanging signaled the end of the noon hour.

"Uh-oh." Cory glanced toward the schoolhouse. "You don't want to be marked tardy. Better hurry."

"I'm going as fast as I can." Andi brushed the fine powder from her sleeves and sneezed again.

Cory bit his lip. "You're awfully dirty, Andi. I wonder what the teacher will say."

"I know what my father will say." Virginia weaved her way through the cluster of students watching the game. She put her hands on her hips and sniffed her disgust. "He'll say he's never seen such a dreadful sight. Then he'll most likely send her home from school."

Andi's stomach clenched. How like Virginia to pop up at the most inconvenient times. Her words stung, mostly because they were true. The schoolmaster was going to take a dim view of her unladylike behavior, and it was her own fault.

"You needn't rub it in." She shook the dust from her braids.

Virginia stepped forward, wrinkling her nose. "You look like one of those dirty little beggar boys I used to see in the city, roaming the streets and picking through the garbage. A shame, really. You come from a fine family."

Andi glared at Virginia. She knew she should turn and walk away. The second bell would ring at any minute, and she didn't want to be marked tardy. But she didn't move.

Neither did any of the other pupils. Who wanted to miss this show-down?

It looked like the entire class would be marked tardy today.

"You gonna let her insult you like that, Andi?" Johnny called out.

Andi wanted nothing more than to rub Virginia's lying face in the dirt, but she didn't. A young lady did not rub another young lady's nose in the dirt—no matter what. Not even if she lied or said unkind things. A young lady always exhibited self-control, especially if her family name was Carter.

Andi drew a deep breath, calmed her pounding heart, and pretended Virginia's words meant nothing to her. She looked her in the eye and said, "I guess I'd rather be a dirty beggar than a liar."

Virginia's face flamed. Then *smack*. She slapped Andi across the face.

Andi's hand flew to her stinging cheek. She gaped at Virginia in astonishment. Then the hot, sick feeling in her stomach boiled over and engulfed her. She forgot her promise to her mother. She forgot she was a young lady. She forgot she was a member of a respected family.

With a cry of outrage, Andi flew at Virginia and knocked her to the ground.

Virginia shrieked. A gasp went up from the watching students. Johnny laughed. Cory groaned.

Andi slammed Virginia onto her back and sat on her just like her brothers would straddle a stubborn calf. "Don't you ever hit me again," she said in a low voice. "Don't lie to me. And stop getting me into trouble with your father."

Virginia thrashed and tossed her head from side to side. "You're crushing me," she whimpered. "I can't breathe. I'm going to be sick. Let me up." One flailing hand caught Andi's dress bodice and ripped away part of the lace trim. It dangled in Virginia's face.

Andi held her down. "Not until you—"

"Stop it, Andi!" Cory grabbed her arm and dragged her away from Virginia. "The teacher's coming."

Indeed, a glowering Mr. Foster was striding purposefully across the schoolyard. "The tardy bell has rung. Why has no one returned to class?" He pushed his way through the crowd of gawking students. "You will all be marked tardy if—"

He stopped short at the sight of Andi and Virginia sprawled on the ground. Both girls were covered in dust. Virginia was sobbing.

Mr. Foster stood speechless. Then with a low moan, he flung himself beside his daughter.

Virginia clutched at her father and wailed.

The schoolmaster found his voice. "What is the meaning of this display? Two young ladies—my *daughter*—sitting in the dirt. For shame! Rise at once and return to the schoolroom." He rounded on the other students and roared, "All of you. Back to class."

Andi scrambled to her feet, breathing hard. Virginia rose shakily, took a few halting steps, and staggered against her father. "She called me a liar," she said between sobs. "She attacked me and sat on me and was beating—"

"You *are* a liar," Andi cut in.

"Enough!" Mr. Foster held Virginia close. "I have eyes, and I know very well who's to blame for this incident. Now, get back to class."

Andi dashed away. Her chest and throat were tight from holding back tears. Her eyes stung. She pushed past her classmates, pounded up the porch steps, and took the narrow stairs two at a time. Then she flung herself into her seat and buried her head in her arms.

The rest of the students found their seats. "Oh, Andi," Maggie whispered from a few rows away, "Mr. Foster's awful mad."

"Yeah, you're really gonna get it." Johnny almost sounded sorry.

"Glad I'm not you," Jack piped up from the seat behind her.

Andi ignored them all.

Mr. Foster arrived a few minutes later, supporting a hobbling Virginia. Andi raised her head and watched him settle the girl in her desk. She was no longer crying, but her face was streaked with muddy tears. Her pale hair tumbled around her face in wild tangles. She did, indeed, look pitiful.

The schoolmaster walked to the front of the room and turned to face his class. "I have never, in all my years of teaching, been witness to such a sight as I saw today. It is a disgrace that a young lady under my instruction should behave in such an unseemly manner."

Andi ducked her head.

"Andrea Carter, you make a mockery of your family's good name and their position in this town. You are unruly, short-tempered, and lack any shred of self-control. You have bullied another student, without thought for her delicate constitution. I have no choice but to punish you."

Andi swallowed. She felt sick at the teacher's words—sick, ashamed, and angry. But mostly she was angry. Why was she being singled out when Virginia was also guilty? Her temper flared, and the warm rush of blood to her cheeks loosened her tongue. "It's true I knocked her down, Mr. Foster. But Virginia slapped me first."

"That's right!" Cory added his support. "Virginia was doing her own share of mean-mouthed name-calling, and Andi never touched her."

"Why don't you be fair and punish 'em both?" Jack hollered.

Andi's spirits rose—a little.

Mr. Foster snatched his ruler and brought it down across his desk with a mighty *whack*, and it broke in two. He shook the broken half at Cory and Jack. "Enough." He tossed the ruler aside and looked at Andi. "A well-bred young lady does not attack a schoolmate— especially another young lady—no matter what the provocation."

He stepped to the corner and picked up a long, narrow switch. "Since you have behaved like a rowdy boy, I have no choice but to punish you like one."

Andi's anger melted into fear. Not the switch! No girl had felt the schoolmaster's switch. She did not want to be the first. Why, oh why had she let her temper take over? Virginia's slap was nothing more than a bee sting. *Why didn't I walk away?*

Worse, what would Mother say?

Mr. Foster held up the switch. "Rise and pass to the front, Miss Carter."

Andi jerked back to the here and now. Her throat went dry. She couldn't go up there. She wouldn't. No mean-spirited teacher was going to hit her with a stick. Especially not in front of the entire class. "P-please, Mr. Foster," she stammered, "couldn't you send a note home instead?"

"Certainly not. I handle my own disci—"

"Leave her alone." The command from the back of the room crackled with annoyance.

Every head turned. Chad stood near the stairwell, tall and unsmiling, with his arms folded across his chest. His set jaw and icy blue glare shouted his anger.

Andi stared at her brother, numb with shock. What was he doing here?

Mr. Foster frowned. "This is none of your affair, Mr. Carter. The school board put me in charge of this classroom, and I intend to discipline this student as she deserves."

"With that?" Chad made his way to the front of the room and pointed to the switch in Mr. Foster's hand. "I don't care what she's done. Nobody touches my sister with a stick. *Nobody.*"

"The school board—of which your brother is a trustee—gives me the right to do just that. Are you challenging their decision?"

Chad plucked the switch from Mr. Foster's hand. "I reckon I am." He snapped it in two and tossed the broken pieces onto the schoolmaster's desk. Then he marched up the aisle. When he got to Andi's desk, he gave her a grim smile. "Come on, Andi. We're leaving."

"Your meddling in my classroom will not go unaddressed at the next school-board meeting, and"—he raised his voice—"your sister is expelled."

Andi gasped. *Expelled!* Being kicked out of school was a disgrace reserved for the most unruly of pupils.

Murmurs of shock and sympathy rippled through the room.

Chad shrugged. "Suit yourself." He took Andi by the arm and steered her toward the stairs. "C'mon, let's get out of here."

Chapter Ten

CONSEQUENCES

"Y ou should see yourself," Chad remarked as soon as they were alone. He stood on the schoolhouse porch and lifted the torn bit of trim dangling from Andi's dress. "You're not a pretty sight." He shook his head, released the lace, and clattered down the steps. "Want to tell me what happened?"

Andi hurried after her brother and gave him a quick account of the noon hour. "And then you showed up," she finished breathlessly, coming up beside him. "What were you doing at school? Not that I'm not grateful, mind you. It was just such a surprise to see you."

Chad grinned and kept walking down the wooden sidewalk. "A nice surprise, I bet."

It was true. Andi had felt utterly alone when she faced her angry schoolmaster. Chad's unexpected appearance had made her feel warm and safe. She knew he was still upset about his stallion, yet he'd come to her rescue—no questions asked.

Yes, she decided, sometimes it's mighty nice having a big brother, even a bossy one. She grabbed his hand and squeezed. "Thanks, Chad."

Chad ruffled her hair. "I couldn't stand there and let him wallop you, now could I? Not my sweet, pretty, innocent little sister." Now he was teasing. Andi wasn't innocent, and they both knew it.

They crossed a street near the edge of town. "So, why did you really come by today? And don't say it was just to rescue me."

81

"Good timing, wasn't it?" He laughed and got down to business. "I needed you and Rosa to stop by the lumberyard after school to catch a ride home. I reckon I'll have to send someone back for Rosa this afternoon." He sighed. "You sure know how to complicate my life."

Andi stopped in her tracks. "Why can't Justin take us home? He didn't go to Sacramento again, did he?"

Chad shook his head. "Not this time. He went to Merced."

Andi looked at him blankly.

"For the murder trial, remember? Justin's defending that drifter, Jed Hatton. The one who killed the baggage clerk over at the depot last month." He paused. "Just before school started."

"Oh, *that* trial." Andi shivered, a delicious, scary shiver. The killing of old Mr. Slater had thrown the town of Fresno into a hanging frenzy. Even the children were caught up in it. Justin might think Jed was innocent, but the rest of the town sure didn't.

No, Jed Hatton was the likely suspect, and Andi had been as disappointed as the rest of the town when the trial was moved safely away to the north. "It sure would be interesting to sit in court and watch Justin try to prove that Jed didn't kill Mr. Slater, wouldn't it?"

"I suppose," Chad replied. He started walking.

Andi scurried to catch up. "What's the matter? Don't you think he'll win?"

"Oh, our brother's pretty good in the courtroom, no doubt about it. He might be able to save Jed's scrawny neck." He shrugged. "I just can't figure out why he's defending Jed in the first place."

Andi slowed her pace. "Justin says Jed's innocent until proven guilty. He told me folks have listened to gossip and stirred themselves up to think otherwise." She glanced up at her brother. "Do you suppose Justin's right?"

Chad shook his head. "Sorry, Andi, but I don't agree with Justin on this one. I think Jed's as guilty as they come." He grasped Andi's sleeve and gave her a tug. "Either way, it's not your concern. You've got your own set of worries"—he chuckled—"like facing Mother this afternoon."

Not funny! Andi groaned.

They reached the lumberyard, where Mitch was stacking an assortment of planks and two-by-fours onto a buckboard wagon. Chad waved. "Looks like it's about loaded up, little brother."

"No thanks to *you*." Mitch wiped the sweat from his forehead. "You sure took your time getting back."

"Something came up."

"Like what?" He glanced at Andi, who was leaning against the buckboard in gloomy silence. "What are you doing here?"

Chad grinned. "I had to rescue our little sister from being thrashed by the new teacher." Now that it was over, he certainly seemed to be enjoying the retelling.

Andi wasn't.

Mitch stared at her. "Your teacher was going to thrash you? Why?"

Andi didn't answer. Instead, she climbed over the wheel and slumped against the stack of lumber.

"I rescued her in the nick of time." Chad lifted a bucket of nails into the back. "Go ahead and tell him what you told me, Andi. It's a pretty good story. And no more than that lying Foster girl deserves, if you ask me."

"Nobody's asking you," Andi grumbled. But at Chad's urging, she told Mitch what had happened.

By the time she finished her story, Mitch was laughing. He wiped the tears from his eyes and leaned against the buckboard for support. "You sat on her?"

"It's not funny," Andi insisted.

"Not if you don't think so, Sis," Mitch agreed, suppressing a smile. He picked up a length of rope and tossed it to Chad, who waited on the other side of the rig.

From her spot on top of the lumber, Andi watched her brothers tie down their load. They didn't appear concerned about what would happen when she arrived home.

Andi, however, was growing more anxious by the minute. No matter how carefully she gave an account of the incident, her mother wasn't likely to understand. But if one of her brothers was willing to explain, maybe—

"Hey, Chad!" She jumped up in her excitement, nearly losing her balance. She caught the back of the seat to steady herself. "Maybe you or Mitch could explain to Mother about my being expelled. I could study my lessons at home. I'd do loads of chores for punishment. You know, like checking fences, flushing out strays, brushing the horses, and washing the surrey."

Chad shook his head. "Sorry, Andi, but you're talking to the wrong brothers. You need a smooth-tongued lawyer to help you out of this fix, and Justin's gone for the week." He secured the rope with one final tug and climbed onto the seat. Grabbing the reins, he released the brake.

"Come on, Mitch. Let's forget the rest of our business in town and go home. I'm sure our sister is eager to break the news to Mother."

Andi wasn't eager for any such thing. However, because she didn't want her mother learning about this newest trouble from her teacher, she determined to tell her the first chance she got.

She settled herself between her brothers on the buckboard's wooden seat and concentrated on how she could break this news without making it sound as bad as it was. She practiced the words in her head over and over until the wagon pulled into the yard.

"Hop out," Chad said cheerfully.

For once, the ride home hadn't been long enough.

Within minutes, Andi was sitting on her bed, pouring out the details of her quarrel with Virginia and its disastrous conclusion. When she finished, she held her breath and watched her mother's face for a reaction.

"I thought we agreed you were going to get along with Virginia," Mother said.

"I tried." Andi felt close to tears. Mother seemed so disappointed in her. "I really tried. But when she slapped me, I just . . . well, I lost my temper." She bowed her head. "I'm sorry, Mother."

"I'm sure you are."

"There's one more thing. Please don't be angry." Andi swallowed. "I've been expelled."

Mother let out a tired sigh. "Oh, Andrea."

The tears Andi had held back all day began to trickle down her cheeks. "What am I going to do?"

Mother gathered Andi in her arms and held her close. She waited quietly until Andi stopped crying. Then she stroked her hair. "There's only one thing to do, sweetheart. You have to apologize to Mr. Foster for your behavior."

Andi was silent for a moment. Then she nodded. "I can do that."

"You also need to apologize to Virginia," her mother added softly.

"Mother!" Andi sat up straight. "Virginia slapped me first."

"But you chose the easy way—fighting her back—instead of letting it go. Sometimes it takes more courage *not* to fight." She lifted Andi's chin and smiled at her. "Apologizing is the right thing to do. That will take courage too."

Before Andi could reply, Mother rose from the bed. "I'll take you to school in the morning and try to straighten this all out. I'm sure your teacher is a reasonable man, once he's had time to let things settle."

"I hope so," Andi said fervently.

"However," her mother finished, "if Mr. Foster allows you to return to school, you will wear your best clothes for the remainder of the week."

Andi groaned. "My best? I can't do that. I won't be able to play ball or jump rope or do anything. I'll have to sit still all week and worry about spoiling a fancy party dress."

"I know it will be difficult," Mother said, "but I believe that having to care for your clothes will make you stop and think the next time you find yourself in a similar situation."

Andi sighed, defeated. A young lady all week! How would she ever manage it?

"Mr. Foster?" Mother's voice rang clear and strong in the early morning silence of the classroom.

The schoolmaster glanced up from where he sat correcting papers. "Good morning, Mrs. Carter," he replied pleasantly. With a few quick strides, he made his way up the aisle.

He grasped her hand. "I had a feeling I'd be hearing from you, although I confess I didn't think it would be this soon."

"Andrea needs to return to class, Mr. Foster."

"I understand." He looked at Andi. "However, I usually do not allow expelled students back into the classroom until I've met with the school board to discuss the matter."

"Justin has gone to Merced for a trial," Mother explained. "It will be at least a week before he returns and the board can meet. In the meantime, I prefer that Andrea not miss school."

Mr. Foster pulled at his lip, clearly pondering.

"When the board meets, and if they support your decision, then I will be happy to make other arrangements," Mother said. "But for now"—she inclined her head in Andi's direction—"Andrea has something she'd like to say."

"Indeed? It must be something important, seeing that she dressed up for the occasion."

Andi stared at the floor. No amount of pleading had changed her mother's mind about the clothes she had to wear to school today. She'd put on her best blue satin frock, complete with the required number of hot, scratchy petticoats. She'd brushed and combed her hair to her mother's exacting standards.

Now she stood uneasily before the teacher, armed with a carefully worded apology. She locked her fingers behind her back and prayed for the awkward moment to pass.

"Andrea," Mother prompted.

Andi raised her head and met the teacher's dark eyes. "I'm sorry I lost my temper and knocked Virginia down yesterday. It was wrong of me. I promise it won't happen again. May I please return to school?"

Mr. Foster didn't reply to Andi's request. "Mrs. Carter," he said instead. "I do not appreciate your son meddling in my classroom."

"I understand," Mother agreed with a solemn nod. "Chad believed he was protecting his sister, but he could have been more diplomatic about it."

Andi looked at her mother in bewilderment. *Diplomatic! With a stick hanging over my head?* "Mother—"

Mother silenced her with a look. Then she turned back to the schoolmaster. "Do you wish to discipline her now?"

Andi's mouth dropped open. *"Mother!"* She couldn't be serious.

Mr. Foster appeared as astonished as Andi at the offer. "Thank you, Mrs. Carter. I appreciate your cooperation." He folded his arms across his chest and smiled, something Andi had seen him do only once or twice since school started. "However, I don't believe that will be necessary. It appears your punishment more than fits the crime."

He turned to Andi. "Yes, Miss Carter, I accept your apology. For now, you may return to school."

"Thank you," Andi muttered. Mr. Foster was obviously enjoying her discomfort.

Mother returned the schoolmaster's smile. "I can assure you that Andrea's behavior in class this week will be exemplary. Good day, Mr. Foster."

"Good day, Mrs. Carter, and thank you."

Mother left, leaving Andi alone to face the embarrassment of her classmates' stares as they filed into the schoolroom. *This is definitely not going to be a good week*, she decided, scratching at a particularly hot and itchy spot on her leg.

She bit her lip and prepared to endure the next four days, until she would finally be freed from her prison of ruffles and lace.

Chapter Eleven

NEWS

W ith relief bordering on tears, Andi pulled on her regular school clothes the following Monday. She glanced toward her open wardrobe and gave her party frocks a mock salute. "*Adiós, and good riddance.*" She crossed over to the small vanity and brushed out her hair, tying part of it back with a length of blue ribbon.

"Andi Carter," she announced to her cheerful reflection, "you have just been paroled."

She gave an approving glance around her room. For once, it was neat and clean. No dirty clothes or forgotten horse tack lay in a corner. The top of her dresser was tidy and the drawers were closed. She drew back the curtains and opened the doors onto the balcony. A pleasant fall breeze blew across her face.

Andi left her room and skipped down the hallway. She paused at the top of the stairs. The banister beckoned to her. She ran her hand along the polished wooden railing and sighed. *One time*, she reasoned.

"Don't you dare!" Melinda called from her bedroom doorway. She hurried over. "You know how it upsets Luisa. She's certain you're going to break an arm or a leg with all that sliding."

Andi peered down the wide staircase. The Carters' fiery little housekeeper was nowhere in sight. Before Melinda could stop her, she settled herself on the railing and sailed down in happy abandon.

Her delight turned to unexpected pain a moment later when she landed on the foyer floor with a resounding *thud*.

"Ouch!" Andi scrambled to her feet and rubbed her sore backside.

"Serves you right," Melinda scolded from the top of the stairs. She grinned. "But it did look like fun."

Both girls were giggling when they entered the dining room.

"Good morning." Andi beamed.

"Are you responsible for the loud noise we just heard?" Mother asked, sipping her coffee.

Andi pulled out a chair and sat down. "Yes, Mother. I couldn't resist. I woke up so happy, I had to slide, just this once."

"Your prison sentence is over, I see," Chad said.

"You bet it is. Never have I spent a longer week in school. But Mr. Foster smiled at me twice and remarked on my improved character." She scooted her chair closer to the table and reached for her milk. "I think he was surprised to learn I'd actually apologized to Virginia."

Melinda sat down next to Andi. "So, you and Virginia are on good terms?"

"Not exactly. I apologized like I was supposed to, but she wouldn't forgive me." Andi shrugged. "I don't care. I'm just going to make sure I do the right thing from now on." She took a long drink of milk and glanced around the table for something to eat.

Her gaze landed at the head of the table. "Justin, you're home at last. Could you please pass the eggs?"

Justin didn't respond. He was staring intently at the cup of coffee in his hand.

"Yoo-hoo. Justin," Andi repeated a little louder. He looked up. "The eggs, please?"

"Oh, I'm sorry. Here you go." He passed her the heaping platter of scrambled eggs. "I heard you had an interesting week at school," he commented before going back to contemplating his coffee cup.

Mother must have told him everything the second he got home.

"It was a terrible week," Andi said. She slid a generous portion of eggs onto her plate. "Maggie and Rachel wore me out with all their silly admiration. I would have gladly swapped clothes with them if I could've gotten away with it."

She spared a quick glance at her mother, who smiled and continued with her breakfast. "Cory had a conniption fit when he saw I wasn't going to be any good for his ball game. He really got sore when his team lost every game. And that horrid Johnny Wilson teased me and pulled my hair a dozen times. He is such a bully. I wish he—" She broke off. Justin obviously wasn't listening.

"Hmm," he finally remarked. He stared out through the French doors leading to the patio.

Andi followed his gaze. "Is something wrong, Justin?" It wasn't like her big brother not to listen to her tales with both ears wide open.

"Is it the trial?" their mother asked softly.

Justin put down his coffee cup and nodded. "The verdict has been eating away at me since I left Merced. I didn't sleep much last night."

"Jed Hatton was convicted?"

"Yes." He closed his eyes and sighed.

Andi ate her breakfast in silence, listening to every word. She was sorry her brother had lost his case. He looked tired and sad.

"Come on, Justin," Chad said impatiently. "You did your job the best you could. The jury made the decision. It's not your fault." He helped himself to more eggs. "Besides," he added with a smug look, "I always figured Jed was guilty."

"Oh, you did, did you?" Justin's voice turned bitter. "I still believe he's innocent. His trial was about as fair as a lynch mob. Public opinion had him hung before the trial ever began." He shook his head. "I tore the witness's story apart. I should have been able to convince the jury, yet they found him guilty."

"Don't kick yourself," Mitch broke in. "What more could you have done? He got the best lawyer in California, didn't he?"

"Will he hang?" Andi burst out. Wouldn't that be something to tell the kids at school!

"Andrea, that will do," Mother said.

Justin turned to his sister. "No, he won't hang. The judge sentenced him to life in prison."

"There you go," Chad insisted. "With any other lawyer he'd probably have gotten the noose. You saved his worthless hide. Jed should be down on his knees in thanks—"

A loud knock at the front door interrupted the breakfast conversation. Everyone turned when the sheriff walked into the dining room.

"Russ!" Chad greeted him. "Pull up a chair. You're just in time for breakfast."

Sheriff Tate shook his head. "Not this morning." He turned to Justin. "I hate to tell you this, but Jed Hatton escaped last night on his way to prison."

"Last night?" Justin exclaimed. "Where is he now?"

"Nobody knows for sure. He overpowered a guard and stole his weapon. Rumor has it that he's headed this way. Gus Malloy says he spotted him just before dawn on the road leading to town. "

Justin looked stunned. "He's *armed*? How did they let that happen? That's not good."

"No, it's not," the sheriff agreed.

"But why would he come here?" Melinda asked.

Sheriff Tate shrugged. "Who knows? Maybe he wants to make trouble for the witness who spoke against him."

"I told him I was going to appeal," Justin said. "Why couldn't he be patient?"

"He won't stand a chance in an appeal if he comes back to Fresno hunting trouble," the sheriff growled. He turned to Mitch and Chad. "You boys got time this morning to help search the town? I want to make sure he's not here before I do anything else."

"A couple of things around here can't wait," Chad replied. "But we'll join you as soon as we can."

"Fine. Join me when you can." Russ replaced his hat. "Better be on my way. Good morning, ladies. See you boys later."

Chad threw down his napkin and stood up. "Well, little brother," he said to Mitch, "looks like a busy day. Let's take care of things so we can get to town." He nodded to the family. "See you this evening, Mother, girls."

"'Bye," Mitch said. They left in a hurry.

Justin drained the rest of his coffee in one gulp. "I'd better head into Fresno early this morning. I don't intend to let this town string Jed up."

"Sheriff Tate won't stand for a lynching," Mother reminded him.

"I hope you're right." He looked at Andi. "Are you and Rosa ready to go?"

Andi sat up at the question and glanced down at her partially eaten breakfast. She'd been so intent on listening that she'd forgotten all about eating. She scooped up a forkful of eggs. "Can you wait a couple of minutes?"

"Not this morning. You heard the sheriff. I'm leaving right now. Perhaps you and Rosa can ride Taffy and Pal into town."

"What a great idea!" Andi exclaimed. "Could we, Mother?"

"I don't know, Andrea. It's a long way for you girls."

"Please? Justin thinks it's a good idea."

Justin nodded. "I'll make arrangements with Sam Blake to board the horses for the day."

"All right." Mother gave in. "But no shortcuts through anyone's orchards or fields. You stay on the road."

"Yes, ma'am," Andi quickly agreed.

She didn't understand why Mother was always so reluctant to let her ride into town. Andi rode all over the ranch for miles on end, and Mother never said a word against it. It practically took a miracle, though, to be allowed to ride into town on her own.

"I think you should leave early for work more often," she suggested to Justin.

"What? You'd trade my company for that of a horse?" The corners of his mouth turned down in a sad frown. "I'm very hurt."

Andi giggled. "Don't try to make me feel guilty. I never have enough time to ride Taffy these days."

"You're right, honey," Justin agreed with a wink. "Have a wonderful time."

Chapter Twelve

UNWELCOME VISITOR

Andi's joy knew no bounds at the idea of riding Taffy into town. She expressed her delight by challenging Rosa to a horse race. Rosa gritted her teeth and nodded. Andi knew her friend's willingness to race was a sign of true loyalty. To show her gratefulness, she gave Rosa a ten-minute head start.

The road along the valley floor was straight and flat—perfect for racing. Andi galloped toward town in typical breakneck fashion, shouting and laughing and singing at the top of her voice. The memory of her past miserable week melted away, replaced with the pleasure of just being alive on such a beautiful fall morning.

Andi caught up with Rosa less than a mile from town. "You and Pal nearly won." She laughed. "No more head starts."

Rosa rubbed Pal's neck. "He ran, and I hung on."

The girls slowed their mounts and trotted down the street to Blake's livery stable, where the horses would be boarded for the day.

Cory called to the girls as they were leaving the livery. "Wait a minute, and I'll walk with you." He snatched up his books and lunch pail and ran to catch up. "I see you rode—or rather, raced—Taffy to town." He nodded toward the sweaty horses. "Pa will charge your folks extra for the rubdown, you know."

Andi stepped into the sunshine. "It's worth it. I had a fine ride."

"Lucky," Cory said. "How did you talk your ma into letting you ride to town?"

"You'll never believe it!" Andi told him about the sheriff's visit to the ranch.

"Jed Hatton!" Cory's eyes lit up. "Guilty? And escaped? This is the most exciting news around here since Frank Williams found that forty-ounce gold nugget up at Coarse Gold Gulch last spring."

Andi agreed.

Then Cory's smile turned to a frown. He sighed. "I reckon they'll catch ol' Jed today while we're in school. We'll miss all the excitement, like always. Maybe I'll play hooky and join the search."

"You better not," she warned, tugging on his sleeve. Then she grinned. "I hear the first bell. I'll race you to school."

All three took off at a run. They were laughing and gasping for breath when they hit the porch of the schoolhouse and started up the stairs to the classroom.

By the time the second bell rang out its warning to tardy students, Andi was seated quietly beside Rosa. She folded her hands, placed them on her desk, and gave the teacher a cheerful smile when he passed her seat.

This week, she determined silently, *Mr. Foster will find no fault with my behavior.*

"Class will come to order," Mr. Foster announced, stepping to the front of the schoolroom. He opened the day with prayer and his customary reading of a psalm. "'I will lift up mine eyes unto the hills, from whence cometh my help. . . .'" As usual, his droning voice ruined what should have been an inspiring portion of Scripture.

Mr. Foster closed the Bible and announced the morning's first assignment. "Take out your history books and open to page ninety-eight. You will copy the text found in quotes into your copybooks. As always, I expect your best effort, your neatest penmanship."

Andi pulled the two books from her desk and frowned. Penmanship assignments were a sore trial. So far this term, only two pages had met Mr. Foster's exacting standards. Usually, she let her fingers form the tedious letters while her thoughts traveled far away, resulting in a number of unsightly inkblots.

Today I'll pay attention, Andi promised herself. She found her place, dipped her pen into the inkwell, and began to copy the words as neatly and carefully as she could.

"Four score and seven years ago . . ."

Her fingers might cramp writing such a lengthy passage, but she would finish the entire Gettysburg Address without making one mistake!

The minutes dragged by. Even though Andi knew the address by heart, she checked each word in her history book before copying it.

"The world will little note nor long remember . . ."

There was a slight commotion at the back of the room, but Andi would not be distracted. She bent closer to her copybook and kept working. She ignored the rustling skirts and whispers of her classmates.

"That this nation, under God, shall have a new birth of freedom . . ."

Andi's heart swelled. She had only a line or two left to copy, and there were no mistakes!

Cory jabbed her in the back. "Andi," he whispered.

She groaned. A dark, wet blob of ink marred the perfectly formed letters of her last sentence. She spun around. "Cory!" She didn't care if Mr. Foster punished her for her outburst. "You made me ruin my—"

Cory clapped a hand over Andi's mouth and gestured behind his shoulder, toward the back of the room.

Andi glanced past her friend's blond head and stared. Cory removed his hand from her mouth and returned his own gaze to the back of the classroom. Every student sat transfixed, watching the stranger who stood nervously beside the staircase.

The man was tall and heavyset, with dark eyes. Muddy-brown hair fell over his ears. He scratched at his unshaven chin and glanced around the room. With a trembling hand, he pulled a large pistol from the waistband of his pants. "You all sit real still, and nobody'll get hurt."

Andi gulped back her surprise and dug her fingers into Cory's arm. "Don't you know who that is?" she whispered. "It's Jed Hat—"

Cory's hand covered Andi's mouth a second time. "Shh! Don't say nothin' to aggravate him. He's a dangerous killer."

She peeled Cory's fingers from her face and leaned over his desk. "He doesn't look dangerous." She kept her voice low. "He looks scared. You'd be scared too if you were headed to prison for something you didn't do."

"He murdered Mr. Slater," Cory insisted.

"No, he didn't. Justin says he—"

"Enough chatter!" Jed's voice cracked like a rifle shot. "Stop gawkin' and turn around. I ain't no circus freak."

Andi spun around and faced the front of the classroom. She wondered what Mr. Foster was thinking. He sat behind his desk, unmoving, his expression carved from stone. Andi couldn't tell if her teacher's face was white with anger or pale with fright.

Jed grunted and made his way up the aisle toward the schoolmaster. When he reached the front of the room, Mr. Foster rose from behind his desk and confronted Jed. "What is the meaning of this intrusion? These children are under my care. How dare you pull a gun on them! Leave at once."

The stranger looked surprised, but he quickly recovered. He stepped around the desk and backhanded the schoolmaster across the face. Several students gasped. Virginia shrieked. Mr. Foster collapsed into his chair, dazed. Blood trickled from a corner of his mouth.

"I told everybody to sit still and keep quiet. That goes for you too," Jed said. "I got no patience for fools today." He faced the class. "If any of you are thinkin' of makin' a run for it while I'm not lookin', think again. You'll end up like your teacher here."

He pointed a finger at tall, red-haired Seth Atkins. He sat nearest the stairs. "You got any fool notion 'bout leavin', boy?"

"N-no, sir."

"Good." Jed lifted his foot to the seat of an unoccupied desk in the front row. He rested his gun across his knee and seemed to relax. "In case you're wonderin' why I'm here, I'll tell you. The whole town's lookin' for me, and I need a place to hide. They think I killed a fella. Well, I didn't kill nobody, and I ain't gonna let nobody haul me off to prison."

He waved his pistol in the direction of four large windows lining one side of the schoolroom. "This place has got a good view of the town. Nobody can sneak up without me knowin' about it." He crossed to one of the windows and glanced outside. "And if things go sour"—he grinned—"I got me a fine bunch o' hostages."

Andi cringed at the word *hostages*. The more she listened to Jed and watched the way he acted, the less she believed him innocent of killing Mr. Slater. But, she reasoned to herself, fear sometimes did strange things to people. She often used anger to keep others from knowing she was afraid. Perhaps Jed was using meanness to hide his own fear.

Mr. Foster dabbed at his swollen, bloody lip with a handkerchief. "You can't hide in here forever." In spite of his obvious pain and fear, he spoke calmly and sensibly. "The children must be allowed to go home at the end of the day."

"Nobody goes 'til I say so," Jed snapped, "and I say we wait. In a few hours, when they're tired of searchin' the town, I can sneak away. Until then, go on about your business and don't give me no trouble."

Andi swallowed her uneasiness and bent over her copybook. The dried inkblot stared up at her. Her anger at Cory for ruining her perfect page of penmanship now seemed silly. She slammed the copybook shut and reached for her speller.

She couldn't concentrate. Her thoughts were too mixed up to care about the lesson she should be studying. Why had Jed risked coming back to town? He should have run far, far away.

If only Justin were here! He could help Jed. He'd fix everything.

A muffled sob brought Andi out of her musing. Rosa sat hunched over her reader. Two tears splattered onto the page. Andi reached over and patted her friend on the back. "Don't cry, Rosa," she whispered. "I know it doesn't look like it, but Justin says Jed's innocent. He won't hurt us, not so long as we're quiet and do what he says."

Rosa nodded and rubbed her eyes. She gave Andi a halfhearted smile.

Jed circled the room, weaving up and down the aisles like an over-attentive schoolmaster. Each time he passed the windows, he peered cautiously outside. Then, with a sigh and a grunt, he continued making his way around the classroom.

The morning dragged. The pupils had never been so quiet for so long. By midmorning Jed's movements had settled into a mind-numbing routine. The sound of his boots clomping up and down the aisles was a constant reminder of his unwelcome presence. Occasionally, he stopped near a desk, hiked his boot up onto the seat of a frightened boy or girl, and rested his gun hand across his knee.

When Jed stopped at Andi's desk and shoved his booted toe onto her seat, she forced herself to ignore him. *I won't let him frighten me.* She calmly turned a page in her geography book. Jed gave a lock of her hair a quick, painful tweak and moved on.

It was close to noon when Jed completed another dreary circle of the schoolroom. He stifled a yawn and peered out the window, like he had done a dozen times already.

All of a sudden, he uttered a curse and leaped backward. "A couple o' men are headed this way. Looks like that sheriff ain't gonna give up 'til he searches every building, shed, and privy in this town." His dark eyes searched the classroom. "This ain't workin' like I planned," he muttered, pacing the room.

Mr. Foster stood up. "Let me talk to the sheriff's men. I'll tell them there's no need to search the school. You were here, but you left an hour ago. When the men leave, you'll have a chance to make your escape."

Jed stopped his pacing and looked at Mr. Foster with fresh interest. "You serious, Teacher? You'd do that?"

Mr. Foster nodded. "For the children's sake, so you'll leave this classroom." He started for the stairs.

"No!" Virginia leaped from her seat and ran to her father. "Don't leave me, Father!" She threw her arms around his waist and clung to him. "Take me with you."

Jed rushed up the aisle and grabbed Virginia's arm. "Hush, girl." He pressed a rough hand over her mouth and pulled her close. "So, this is your little gal. Ain't that nice."

Mr. Foster drew a shaky hand across his forehead. "Please don't hurt her."

"Just deliver the message."

"I'll be right back, Virginia," he assured her. Then Mr. Foster disappeared down the stairs.

An eerie silence settled over the classroom while they waited for the teacher's return. Virginia trembled in Jed's grasp. Her eyes glistened with tears. A sob caught in her throat.

"I said hush," Jed snapped.

Virginia choked back her tears and looked at Andi.

Andi stared back, horrified at this turn of events. What had come over Virginia to yell "father" in front of Jed? *Do you know what kind of fix you're in now?* she wanted to shout. *You've given Jed the perfect hostage.*

She had a good idea that Virginia knew—too late—the danger she'd put herself into. It made her helplessness all the more heart-wrenching to watch. *Please, God,* Andi prayed silently, *hurry up and bring Mr. Foster back to class, before Virginia dies of fright.*

She squeezed her eyes closed to shut out the look of despair on

Virginia's face, but it was no use. Even behind closed eyelids, Andi easily visualized the girl's plight.

Mr. Foster returned to the classroom a few minutes later. Andi wanted to cry out in relief. Perhaps Jed would leave now.

"Well?" Jed snarled. He kept a tight grip on Virginia. "What happened?"

Mr. Foster kept his attention on his daughter and returned to his desk. "I think they believed me. They asked which way you went. I told them you headed west, toward the railroad depot." He sank into his chair. "You should leave right now, while the search party is—"

"Don't tell me my business!" Jed shoved Virginia away. She ran to her father and threw herself at him, sobbing. Mr. Foster held her close.

Jed moved toward the stairs. Just before he started down, he raised his gun. "You better hope those men believed you, or somebody's gonna be very sorry." He turned and vanished down the narrow stairway.

The classroom broke into noisy, relieved chatter.

"Jed Hatton!" A familiar voice shouted from outside.

Andi's heart leaped with hope. Justin had come! Just as quickly, her heart settled to her stomach in a cold, hard lump.

Now Jed's trapped, she realized. *And so are we.*

Chapter Thirteen

THE PERFECT HOSTAGE

J ed clattered back up the stairs and burst into the classroom. He raced up the aisle, snatched Virginia from her father, and crushed her against his chest.

Virginia gasped.

Mr. Foster reached for his daughter, but Jed shoved him away. "You fixed it for me real good!" He edged his way toward the partly open window and peered out, dragging the sobbing Virginia with him. "They didn't believe you for a minute."

"I don't understand," Mr. Foster protested. "I told them exactly what—"

"Jed Hatton!" Justin shouted a second time. His voice carried clearly into the classroom from the schoolyard below. "It's Justin Carter. I'm unarmed. Let me come up and talk to you. We can work something out."

Listen to him! Andi begged silently. She turned to see what Jed would do. He was trying to watch the classroom, look out the window, and keep control of Virginia, all at the same time. The girl whimpered and twisted and begged to be set free, all the while crying for her father.

Mr. Foster stepped forward.

Jed raised his gun. "Stay put." Then he turned and shouted out the window. "It's no use, lawyer. I know you tried, and I ain't holdin' it against you, but it's too late. You said the jury wouldn't find me guilty, but they did."

"It's *not* too late," Justin argued. "We can appeal. But it won't work with you up there, holding those kids. You've got to give yourself up. Let me help you, Jed. I promise no one will hurt you."

Jed grew silent. He dug his fingers into Virginia's arm. "Hush, girl. I can't think with all that sniveling." He returned to the open window. "Let me study on it a bit."

"All right," Justin agreed. "Take your time."

Jed stared out the window, clearly deep in thought. Then he studied Virginia's pale, tear-streaked face and sighed. His grip on her arm loosened.

Andi's heart slowed down. Jed seemed ready to do the sensible thing. She smiled inwardly. Chad always said Justin could talk a fence post out of the ground. It looked like he could also convince a frightened, innocent man to give his lawyer another chance.

Crash! A bench at the back of the room hit the floor. Someone scrambled over it and clattered down the steps.

Jed whirled. "Come back here!" He fired a shot at the stairway.

A dozen pupils dived under their desks. Others screamed.

Andi sat frozen. Jed did not look sensible now. He looked furious, and scared out of his wits.

"That tears it!" Jed gripped Virginia and shouted at Mr. Foster. "Your girl gets it the next time somebody tries to leave." He poked his head out the window. "I ain't listenin' to any lawyer's clever words. Not anymore. I'm gettin' outta here."

"Jed," Justin pleaded. "Don't do anything rash."

Jed turned away from the window and squeezed Virginia's arm. "You're perfect. The teacher's gal. Just what I need to get outta this town in one piece." He gave her a jerk. "Come on, let's go."

Virginia drew a frantic breath at Jed's words. "No, not me. Oh, please!" She tried to tear herself from his crushing grip. "Father, don't let him take me." She gulped for air. Her voice rose to a shriek. *"Father!"*

Mr. Foster sprang to his feet. "Mr. Hatton, please reconsider. My daughter is not strong. Her health is delicate. She's not used to the roughness of this country. I beg you, sir, don't take her."

Jed dragged Virginia back across the room and jammed his pistol into Mr. Foster's chest. "Sit down an' shut up."

Mr. Foster sat. He didn't say another word, but his fists clenched and unclenched. He looked out of his mind with worry.

"Don't you see I got no choice?" He shook Virginia. "Stop your bawlin' and get hold of yourself." She cried louder. "I mean it, girl. If you don't shut up, I'm gonna slap you."

Virginia's heartbreaking cries for help echoed in Andi's ears. Her chest tightened until she could scarcely breathe. Her stomach turned over.

Andi looked at the teacher. *You're her father!* she screamed silently. *You know she can't go with Jed. Why don't you do something?*

You do something, a quiet voice whispered in her head.

Me? I can't, Andi protested. *I'm just a girl. What can I do? I can't run up and snatch Jed's gun away. I'm scared too. Surely God doesn't expect me to—*

A sharp slap and Virginia's scream yanked Andi from her mental seesaw. She sprang to her feet. "Stop it!"

Jed's hand froze in midair. He spun around and gaped at Andi. Then he dropped his hand to his side. The next slap never came. Virginia fainted. She slumped to the floor and lay in a heap at Jed's feet.

Andi glanced around the room. Everyone was staring at her in astonishment. She was just as surprised as her classmates to find herself the center of attention. She didn't know what to do or say, so she said the first thing that came to her mind.

"Don't take Virginia with you. She'd be no use at all. Look at her. She fainted. She does it all the time. And she can't ride. You wouldn't make it a mile from town before she fell off the horse. That'd slow you down an awful lot."

Andi paused for breath. She knew she was babbling. Her sentences tumbled out, one on top of the other. *Jed's looking at me like I'm a lunatic. What do I do now?*

The answer struck like lightning.

"Take me, instead," she blurted. "I promise I won't cry or faint."

Jed Hatton's mouth fell open.

Andi's unexpected offer brought Mr. Foster to life. "Andrea, sit down." He hurried over to where Virginia lay and rested a protective hand on her head. "Mr. Hatton, none of these children will leave the classroom. I will not allow it. Your only chance—"

The smash of a gun-butt against his head sent the teacher sprawling to the floor next to his daughter. He lay unconscious, blood dripping from a wide cut.

"Interferin' fool," Jed muttered. He returned his attention to Andi. "So, you want to take this ninny's place?"

Andi stared at Jed, tongue-tied with fear. *What have I done?*

She looked at the two unconscious people lying crumpled at Jed's feet and knew exactly what she'd done. It was simple. Virginia was a newcomer to the valley. She knew nothing about surviving out of town.

Virginia was without a doubt the most unlikable, spiteful, and lying girl Andi had ever met, but she was also lonely, fragile, and frightened to death. She didn't deserve to be dragged through the wild by a scruffy, escaped prisoner—even if he *was* innocent.

"Did you hear me, girl?" Jed snapped. "You want to take her place?"

Andi set her jaw. Perhaps she'd been hasty with her decision, but nobody else was jumping in to lend a hand. It looked like it was up to her. Taking Virginia's place was the right thing to do, no matter how scared she was.

She squared her shoulders and faced Jed. "Yes. Take me."

"If that ain't the craziest thing I've ever heard." Jed laughed. "No thanks. I'm better off with this snivelin' little lady, though she'll most likely give me no end of trouble. You got gumption, I'll give you that, but I need somebody important, like this teacher's little gal." He prodded the unconscious girl with his boot toe.

"My brother's your lawyer," Andi snapped. "Is that important enough for you?"

Jed's eyes widened, and he gave a low whistle. "I reckon it is at that." He left Virginia lying on the floor and hurried down the aisle. "You really Justin Carter's sister?" He grinned.

Andi nodded.

"Well, that's mighty fine, girl. Mighty fine. You reckon your brother'll give me what I want when he sees I've got you?"

Andi bristled. "I guess you'll have to ask him and find out."

Jed chuckled. "You're full of sass. That's good." He gripped her arm. "Let's go."

Andi took a deep breath and allowed Jed to steer her to the back of the room and down the stairs. Her stomach lurched in fear. *There's nothing to be afraid of,* she scolded herself. *Jed's innocent. Justin said so. Justin will take care of everything.*

But her stomach continued to churn.

Jed cracked open the schoolhouse doors. "Hey, Carter!"

"I'm listening," Justin said.

Andi peeked through the opening and gasped. Dozens of eager-looking citizens—armed with everything from old shotguns to shiny Winchester rifles and pearl-handled six-shooters—lined the street across from the grammar school. Justin and Sheriff Tate stood in the schoolyard, no more than a dozen yards away.

Jed whistled at the sight. "I'll make this quick, lawyer. I'm holdin' a girl here who says she's your sister. If you got any feelings for her, you clear out all these trigger-happy folks and find us a couple o' horses and some grub. Then me and the little lady'll ride out real peaceful-like."

"No, Jed!" Justin's voice betrayed his shock and dismay. "That's not the answer. Don't destroy your chance for an appeal by doing something so stupid. Your best bet is to throw out your gun and let me come inside and talk to you. I know you're not a killer. We have a chance—a *good* chance. Don't throw it all away because you're scared."

"Quit yer jabberin'. All I want is a couple o' horses and some supplies. Are you gonna get 'em or not?"

"All right," Justin said. "We'll do it."

Jed opened the door wider and poked his head out. "Glad to hear that. I reckon we'll—"

A bullet cracked into the doorpost. It sent splinters of wood into Jed's face and into Andi's hair. Jed slammed the door shut. He reached for Andi and gave her a rough shake. "Is your brother fool enough to want to see you dead?"

"Justin didn't do it!" Andi insisted, stifling a sob.

"Maybe not, but some fool did." He wrapped a shaking arm around Andi and crushed her to his side. Then he kicked open the door. "Lawyer, you nearly got us both shot." He raised his gun and made his way down the porch steps and into the schoolyard. "You keep all these gun-totin' fools away and bring me my horses and supplies, or something bad's gonna happen to this girl."

"Take it easy, Jed." Justin held up his empty hands. "I'm unarmed. That shot was fired by accident. It won't happen again. We're sending somebody for the horses."

Sheriff Tate motioned to a couple of his deputies and whispered his orders. When they took off, he raised his voice to the onlookers. "There's nothing more for you to do here. You folks can go about your business."

Nobody moved. "You hear me?" the sheriff repeated in a louder tone. "Clear out." The crowd reluctantly dispersed.

Andi shaded her eyes against the brightness of the noon sun. Why did Justin look so scared? Her oldest brother was strong and smart. He always had the right answers. He always knew what to do. He'd be able to convince Jed to let her go . . . wouldn't he?

"Justin?" she ventured. He motioned her to be quiet.

Jed was speaking. "Listen, Mr. Carter. I'm sorry it had to be your sister. I grabbed me the teacher's girl—a snivelin' little thing—but she was fixin' to be real trouble. This girl here felt sorry for her and offered to take her place. When she told me she was your sister, I couldn't pass it up."

"Let her go, Jed," Justin ordered.

"Nothin' doin'."

"You don't need her. Take me. I'll go with you for as long as you like. We can talk. Just you and I. When you feel safe, we'll come back together and start the appeal. Or you can leave me along the road and be on your way." He spread his hands in sincerity. "I give you my word."

Jed shook his head. "I've already had me an earful of your fancy words and I don't want no more." He tightened his grip on Andi. "Now, where are those horses?"

Justin's shoulders slumped. "They're on their way."

The next few minutes seemed like an eternity to Andi. Crushed against Jed until she couldn't take a deep breath, she wondered why her brother didn't do anything to help her. He stood scarcely a stone's throw away, yet he made no effort to speak to Jed or to her. In fact, he looked very much like Mr. Foster had looked a few minutes before—frightened and helpless.

Alarmed at the similarities, she burst out, "Justin, why don't you do something?" Then she realized that Mr. Foster had tried to do something, and he was lying unconscious on the schoolroom floor.

"I'm sorry, honey," Justin said softly. "I tried. The only way I can protect you now is by doing exactly what Jed says. As long as you and I remember that, he won't hurt you. You'll be safe." He nodded at Jed. "Isn't that right, Jed?"

Jed grinned. "You betcha. I wouldn't think of hurtin' a hair on this girl's head, so long as she behaves herself and gives me no trouble. I like her. She showed more gumption than anybody else in that schoolroom. We'll get along just fine, I reckon. I might even let her go, once I'm in the clear."

He broke into a broad smile as two horses, led by the sheriff's deputy, were brought to a halt in front of him.

Andi stared at the horses in wonder. She didn't know how the sheriff had arranged it, but Taffy stood next to a paint gelding. She was saddled, bridled, and ready to go. Her spirits rose at this unexpected gift.

"It looks like we'll be headin' out." Jed led Andi to Taffy and tossed her up on the mare's back. To her dismay, Jed pulled himself up behind her and accepted the paint's lead rope. He gripped his gun with his free hand and said, "I ain't takin' no chances, little lady. We ride together for a spell."

Andi twisted around and looked at Jed through tear-filled eyes. "May I please say good-bye to my brother?"

"Make it quick."

Andi's throat tightened when she met Justin's grief-stricken gaze. She blinked to hold back her tears. "I'm sorry I made a mess of things, Justin. Tell Mother I love her. Tell her good-bye for me and . . . and I'll see her soon."

"I will," Justin promised, stepping up to the horse. He ignored Jed's warning look and took Andi's shaking hand. "You did the right thing," he said. "I'm proud of you. Now, don't be afraid. Be strong. Be brave. And God go with you." He gave her hand a gentle squeeze. "Even if I can't."

Andi nodded and tried to speak. She wanted to tell Justin she'd be strong and brave and anything else he wanted her to be, but the words stuck in her throat. Tears came instead.

Jed raised his pistol. "Step aside, counselor."

Justin dropped Andi's hand and backed away. "I love you," he whispered.

Jed yanked Taffy around and urged her into a gallop. It wouldn't be long before Fresno was far, far behind.

Chapter Fourteen

INTO THE UNKNOWN

Jed galloped Taffy until Andi was sure her horse would collapse from exhaustion. She was furious, but it helped push aside her fear. Many miles south of town, Jed finally slowed the horse to a walk, then stopped. He dismounted but hung onto Taffy's reins.

"Listen here," he said. "I'm mountin' up on this paint horse. If you know what's good for you, you'll stay put."

Andi nodded wearily. "Haven't we gone far enough? You've got a good head start. You could go a lot faster without me, you know."

"Shut up," Jed ordered. He mounted the paint horse and jerked Taffy's reins.

The mare leaped forward. Only Andi's ability to react quickly saved her from a nasty spill. She managed to keep her seat, which brought a look of respect from Jed.

"Well, little lady, looks like you were the better choice all the way around. We'll make good time, you and me."

"Don't worry about *me*, mister. I can keep up. But I'm not so sure about the horses. You're pushing them too hard."

Jed barked a laugh and tossed Taffy's reins to Andi. "I'll decide that. Here. Take the reins. But I'm warning you . . ." He laid a hand on the gun in his waistband. "No tricks. You stick close, or else. Understand?"

"Yes," Andi replied through clenched teeth. She gathered up the reins. "I understand perfectly."

Jed reached out and slapped Taffy's rump. "Let's move!"

Taffy took off, with Jed close behind. They rode all afternoon, stopping only long enough to water the horses. Jed led them through scrub oak and gulches filled with thick, scratchy brush. They crossed dry creek beds and urged the horses over hills that grew higher as they neared the mountains. The scorching sun beat down for so long that Andi was sure evening would never come.

"Where are we going?" she asked during one of their brief stops to water the horses. She squatted on the rocks, plunged her hands into the stream, and splashed cool water on her face. Then she drank her fill. She wished Jed would let her take off her shoes and stockings so she could wade, even for a minute. She was sweltering in this heat.

Jed looked at her. "We're goin' to Mexico. But first I gotta lose any posse that might be tailing us."

Andi froze. Water dripped down her face. "Mexico?" Mexico was far from home. Nobody would ever find her there. "I don't want to go to Mexico."

"I ain't askin' you. Now, get outta the water and back on the horse."

"Just a minute more?" she begged. "I'm so hot."

Jed shook his head. "Do like I tell you."

Andi reluctantly left the stream and climbed onto Taffy. Mexico! She shuddered. There had to be some way she could let the posse know which way they'd gone. Their horses were leaving very few tracks over this rocky country.

If only I had something to drop. A handkerchief? A button? Her shoe?

Andi shook her head. Jed always put Taffy in the lead. He followed close behind and watched her too closely to let something as obvious as a shoe fall by the wayside. And she was fresh out of handkerchiefs. Maybe a button?

She reached around to her back and pretended to scratch an itchy spot. Her fingers scraped a button, but Mother was too good a seamstress. The button held fast.

Then something smooth caught between her fingers. Her hair ribbon! Andi yanked. The ribbon didn't budge. She peeked over her shoulder.

Jed was busy tightening his cinch.

It's now or never. Andi reached both hands behind her head and loosened the knot that held back her hair. She balled the ribbon and hid it in her clenched fist. Her hair tumbled around her face, making her hotter than ever.

Jed swung into the saddle and kneed his horse. "Giddup," he barked.

Andi kept Taffy still. As usual, Jed trotted up and slapped the mare's rump. When Taffy leaped forward, Andi let the ribbon fall. She didn't dare look back. Instead, she prayed the blue ribbon would stand out on the rocks and guide her brothers and the sheriff on their search.

They rode silently for many miles. Andi dozed but jerked awake each time Taffy stumbled. It was just as well she didn't fall asleep. A tumble from Taffy would be a painful way to wake up.

Jed trotted up beside her an hour later. He looked at her and sighed.

"What's the matter?" Andi asked. "Why do you keep looking at me like that?"

"Reckon I feel a mite guilty for bringin' you along," Jed confessed. "'Specially after what your brother did for me in court. He's a good lawyer, and he's mighty smart with all those highfalutin words."

He cleared his throat. "But you gotta understand, girl, that I had no choice. I'm innocent. I ain't goin' to prison."

"Justin knows you're innocent," Andi said. "He wants to help you. But running off with his sister is *not* a good way to keep him on your side." She smiled to take the sting from her words. "It's not too late to take me back. It would prove your innocence. You can trust Justin—"

"I can't!" Jed cut her off. "So it's no use tryin' to talk me into turnin' around, or any other fool thing. I'm goin' to Mexico, and you're along to make sure I get there. I'm sorry, little lady, but that's the way it's gotta be. Soon as I cross the border, I'll let you go."

"You're just going to ride off and leave me alone?" Andi was aghast. "Don't you care what happens to me? What kind of a man are you?"

"A desperate one."

By evening, Andi was so tired that she could hardly stay in the saddle. Twice she drifted off to sleep, but the jarring of the horse jerked her awake each time.

Jed looked her up and down. "You're plumb tuckered out, ain't you?" He pulled his horse to a stop near a grove of scraggly cottonwoods and scrub oak and dismounted.

Taffy stopped too. She lowered her head and whickered. Her sides heaved. Andi nearly burst into tears at her horse's poor condition.

"Looks like we can't go no farther tonight," Jed decided, "even if the entire town of Fresno's after us. I hope we've thrown any posse off our trail long enough to get a decent night's rest."

Andi hoped her ribbon had been found. If not, she didn't know how she could keep on going. She slid from the saddle and grabbed the stirrup to keep herself upright.

"This looks as good a place as any," Jed remarked. "Plenty of cover, but enough space to spread out a couple o' bedrolls and graze the horses." He gathered the canteens, saddlebags, and bedrolls into his arms. "Take care of the horses while I set up camp."

Andi didn't move. Take care of the horses? She could barely take care of herself. "B-but the saddles are awful heavy," she stammered.

"Just do it, and do it quick." Jed lugged the gear into the small clearing and dumped everything on the ground. Then he turned back to Andi and planted his hands on his hips. "I'm keepin' you to your promise, remember? No cryin' or faintin' from *you*." He smirked. "Let's see what you Carters are made of."

Jed's mocking words sent a hot rush of blood through Andi that drove her fatigue away, just as he most likely intended. She unsaddled the horses and wrestled with the saddles until the cumbersome pieces of tack were exactly where Jed told her to put them.

Andi collapsed to the ground next to the saddles. She wished with all her heart she could close her eyes, but a weary nicker from Taffy reminded her that she hadn't finished her work.

She dragged herself to her feet and made her way back to hobble the horses and unbridle them. Her fingers fumbled in the growing darkness.

Taffy hungrily attacked the dry autumn grass, snorting her displeasure at the shabby care she was receiving tonight. Andi rubbed Taffy's sweaty neck as the mare bit off quick, short lengths of grass. "I'm sorry. No rubdown tonight," she whispered. "Things will get better soon, though. I promise."

The palomino shook her mane. Andi leaned against her flank and closed her eyes. Taffy was warm, and her presence was a comfort, a reminder of home. The familiar scent and touch of her friend cheered her.

She sighed. *Thank You, God, for sending Taffy along today to keep me company.*

Jed's gruff command yanked Andi from her moment of peace. "Come over here and eat. I don't want you keeling over."

Andi joined her captor. She glanced at the dark shadows creeping over the campsite and shivered. "I don't suppose there'll be a fire."

He laughed. "Sorry, no. Can't take the chance of being spotted."

Andi slid down next to a log and took the food and blanket Jed offered. She bit into the piece of tough beef and made a face. She hated jerky, but tonight she was hungry enough to eat it without choking. Jed passed her the canteen without a word.

Thankful to wash the salty taste from her mouth, Andi drank quickly and handed the canteen back to Jed. Then she drew the blanket around her shoulders, yawned, and closed her eyes.

A rough shake brought her awake with a jolt.

"Hey, girl. I never caught your name."

Andi pulled the blanket closer. "Why do you care?"

"I'm gettin' kinda tired of callin' you 'girl.' Since we're gonna be partners for a spell, I thought we might get on friendlier terms. You can call me Jed if you like."

"No thanks, mister," she mumbled sleepily. "We may be traveling together, but that sure doesn't make us partners."

"Suit yourself," Jed growled. "Just tryin' to be friendly. But I shoulda known. Well, Miss *Carter*, I reckon you'll be mighty glad of my friendship down in Mexico. I know just enough Mexi-talk to get us by."

"You said you were going to leave me at the border."

Jed grinned. "Maybe I changed my mind."

"Go away." Andi was too tired to make sense of Jed's words. "I want to sleep."

"Ain't you the least bit curious to know why I came back to town?"

"No." Andi lay down on the cold, hard ground and curled up into a tight ball. She shivered as the chilly autumn night set in. No moonlight pierced the darkness. Only a handful of stars peeked through the clearing in the trees.

Andi closed her eyes. Never in her life had she felt so cold, tired, or frightened, not even last spring when she'd been locked in that horrible shed for two days. She tried to keep her fear inside, but it trickled out between her eyelids in hot, silent tears.

A whimper escaped her lips. *Please, God. I know Justin said You'd go with me, but I'm so scared. Take care of me, and please help my brothers find me.*

Something or somebody brushed by her. Her eyes flew open. Jed Hatton towered over her, a black shadow against the feeble light of the stars. She caught her breath, frightened to think of what he might do next.

"Don't worry, little lady." He gently covered her with his own blanket and stepped back. "I won't let nothin' bad happen to you."

Andi heard no more.

Chapter Fifteen

A DESPERATE CHANCE

Andi woke with a start and sat up. Dawn was a pale streak in the sky. It took a minute before she remembered where she was and why she'd spent the night on the ground. As the memories washed over her, she shuddered and glanced at her captor.

Jed lay slumped against a large oak tree, snoring. His dirty, unkempt hair hung over his eyes and his gun rested in his lap. His fingers were curled loosely around it.

Andi smiled. Here was her chance to escape. She rose without a sound and made her way over to Taffy, who stood with the paint horse across the campsite. If she could mount Taffy without waking Jed, she would be free. Nobody could catch Taffy.

She whispered quieting words to the mare while she unhobbled her. Grasping the creamy mane, she pulled herself silently onto Taffy's back. With a gentle pressure, she urged her horse forward.

The sharp click of a gun being cocked broke the early morning silence.

Andi froze.

"Goin' somewhere, little lady?"

Andi turned and faced Jed. He was leaning against the tree, groggy from sleep. "I'm going home," came her quiet reply.

Jed yawned and lowered his gun. With a grunt, he rose to his feet and brushed the hair away from his eyes. "Girl," he said, breaking into a grin, "you sure do beat all." He started toward Taffy. "How do you plan on ridin' that horse? No reins, no bridle. You just gonna sweet-talk her into takin' you home?"

"This is *my* horse," Andi said. "She'll go wherever I say."

"Do tell!" Jed chuckled. "I expect we're in for some interestin' times together, you and me. You showed real gumption at the schoolhouse yesterday, but don't let it go to your head. Now, get off the horse."

Andi shook her head. "I want to go home."

"Too bad." Jed scowled. "You listen to me, girl, and listen good. You ain't goin' home. You ain't goin' nowhere 'til I say so." He sighed. "Looks like I'll have to tie you up at night from now on to make sure you stay put."

"Oh no, you won't." Yelling at Jed kept Andi's fear in a corner. "You just wait, Jed Hatton. My brothers will catch up with you. They'll take you back to town and you'll hang, because I betcha anything you really *did* murder that man, no matter what Justin says."

Jed shrugged. With his free hand he fished around inside his jacket and pulled out a small, bulging leather pouch. "Know what this is?"

Andi shook her head.

"It's gold dust. *My* gold dust. The baggage clerk got in the way. I had to kill him." He shook the pouch. "This here's the reason I came back to town. I'd hidden it. I need this gold to live on down in Mexico."

Andi caught her breath. "Then you really *are* guilty!"

Jed smirked. "Yep."

"But Justin—"

"I had him fooled," Jed said. "I admit your brother's a right smart lawyer. He almost got me off. Got me a prison term instead of a noose. Made it easier for me to escape." He laughed. "Kind of a surprise, ain't it?"

Andi's heart slammed against the inside of her chest. She clenched her fists. Jed had lied to Justin, who had done his best to prove the man's innocence. "You low-down, dirty, rotten, lying—"

"Quit your yappin'," Jed ordered. "You can cuss me out all you want later. Let's eat and be on our way."

"Uh-uh. I'm not going another step with a killer who lies to his own lawyer."

Jed marched over to Andi's horse. "You come down off that horse, girl, or I'll pull you off."

"No!" Andi shouted in sudden, frantic decision. She reached out and kicked Jed's gun hand with all her might. The gun flew from his hand and landed on the ground a few yards away. She pressed her heels into Taffy's sides. "Go, Taffy!"

The horse bolted.

Andi heard Jed swear and scramble around for his gun. She paid no attention. She had to ride far and fast.

"Come back here, you fool kid, or I'll shoot. I mean it!"

Never! She'd take her chances. Maybe he was bluffing. She glanced back.

The last thing Andi heard was Jed Hatton shouting at her. The last thing she saw was a bright flash.

Andi woke to the sound of a man's frantic pleading. "You gotta wake up, girl. It was an accident. Just a warning shot. I never meant to hurt you. You gotta believe me." He shook her. "Do you understand? I didn't mean to do it."

Searing pain shot through Andi's head. She tried to make sense of the man's words. What was he talking about? Where was she? Why did everything hurt so much?

"Girl!"

The terror in the man's voice frightened Andi into opening her eyes. A dirty, unshaven face loomed above her. When he saw she was awake, he let out a long, deep sigh and sat back.

"Thank God you're not dead." He lifted Andi's head and stuffed a rolled-up blanket under her. He tucked another blanket around her and rose to his feet. "I hate t' leave you like this, little lady, but I got no choice. Your brother ain't likely to forgive me for this. If I stick around, I'm a dead man." He laid a rough palm against Andi's cheek. His voice softened. "I'm sorry, girl. I really am."

He mounted his horse and galloped away.

No! Don't go! Andi tried to shout, but she couldn't make the words come. She sat up. Pain as sharp as a knife stabbed the inside of her head, making her gasp. She clutched her head with both hands.

Her stomach heaved at the movement. The next moment, what was left of her meager supper spewed on the ground in front of her. She swallowed and took a deep breath. Then another. She lowered her hands and was shocked to see the fingers of her left hand covered in bright-red blood.

What happened? It hurt so much to think. Fighting back another wave of nausea, she glanced around the campsite.

The scruffy-looking man had certainly left in a hurry. A saddle lay abandoned under a tree. Saddlebags and blankets were scattered across the ground. A canteen hung suspended from the branch of a half-dead scrub oak.

"Why did he leave? Where am I?" Andi squeezed her eyes shut and tried to think. But it was no use. Her mind could focus on nothing but the agony inside her head.

She couldn't remember where she was or how she got here, or who the man on the galloping horse was. In fact, she couldn't remember anything at all. It was as if someone had slammed a door shut in her head and locked it tight.

A sharp *crack* from the bushes across the campsite propelled Andi to her feet, heart pounding. She cried out and collapsed to the ground. Her stomach roiled. She scuttled backward into the brush and waited, clenching her teeth against the pain.

To her astonishment, a golden horse broke into the clearing. She trotted up to Andi and nickered a greeting. Then the mare lowered her head and blew out, gently nibbling Andi's hair and nuzzling her in a way that made her feel warm all over.

The joy of finding another living creature made Andi forget her pain for the moment. She crawled from her hiding place and reached up to stroke the mare's soft nose. "I don't know where you came from, but I'm glad you're here."

The horse whinnied and nudged her, as if encouraging her to stand and mount up.

Andi staggered to her feet and leaned against the horse for support. Her head throbbed. "I can't," she apologized, sliding to the ground. "You're too tall."

She knew she should try to find help, yet all she wanted to do was lie down so her head would stop pounding. "Don't wander off," she told the mare. Then she reached for the blankets, crawled into the brush, and curled up on the ground.

Immediately, the pain lessened. With a sigh, she closed her eyes and slept.

Something startled Andi awake. The sun was no longer overhead. Dusk had settled in, casting long, gray shadows over the campsite.

Hoofbeats. Lots of them. Andi sat up at the sound.

It was a mistake. Her head began pounding again. But at least her stomach didn't protest. She looked around for the horse and found her munching on dry grass several yards away. The mare was half-hidden in the shadows. For that, Andi was grateful. She huddled on the blanket and waited to see what would happen.

The sound of hoofbeats grew nearer, then stopped.

"This way," a loud voice boomed. "It looks like they made camp here last night. At least we're on the right track."

There was a rustling sound, and five men appeared in the clearing. Andi watched them from her secluded spot in the brush. None resembled the scruffy man who had abandoned her. These men were strangers.

"What happened here?" A tall man wearing a sheriff's badge yanked the canteen from the deadwood. "Looks like they left in a hurry. Why would they leave all this behind?"

No one answered him.

"Over here!" the sheriff's deputy hollered. "I found a horse. It's the palomino."

Andi didn't know what to do. They'd found the mare. It wouldn't be long before they found—

"Andi!"

The astonished voice just beyond the brush brought her around. She locked gazes with a sandy-haired young man.

He grinned. "I'm sure glad to see *you*. Come on out and tell us what happened. Where's Jed?" He reached out a helping hand and called to the others. "Over here, Justin, Chad!"

Andi shrank away from the man's offer. Things were happening too fast. Who were these people? Who was Jed?

"What's the matter?" The young man's smile faded. He caught his breath. "Justin! There's blood all over the place."

Another man hurried over. His gaze swept over the scene, and his jaw tightened.

"Go away," Andi whispered to this newest intruder.

He backed off. "Take it easy, honey. We didn't mean to frighten you. We've come to take you home."

Home? Andi stared at him. He looked vaguely familiar, but she couldn't place him. *I should know him*, she thought. *But it's too much work to remember.*

"Does your head hurt?" he asked.

"Yes."

"Could I take a look at it? I'll be very careful. I promise." He smiled and reached out his hand. "Let me help you."

Andi considered. She knew she couldn't hide in the bushes any longer. Night was coming on, and she hurt. This man had a gentle voice. She relaxed and placed her hand into his.

He guided her into the clearing and kneeled down beside her. Carefully, he brushed aside the dark, blood-soaked tangles of her hair. "You've got a nasty gash and it's bleeding."

The others crowded around for a closer look.

A man with black hair drew in a sharp breath. "He shot her, Justin." His voice shook with anger. "Your *innocent* client shot our sister. What kind of man would—" He broke off. "I'll kill him myself."

Andi whimpered.

"Take it easy, Chad," Justin warned. "You're scaring her."

"I'm sorry, little sister," Chad said softly. "I didn't mean to scare you." He smiled at her.

Andi wrinkled her forehead. *Little sister?* These men were her brothers? Why didn't she recognize them?

"Did Jed shoot you?" Justin asked.

Andi shivered. "I don't know." She turned a frightened gaze on him. "I don't remember anything." She started to cry. "I only know my head hurts and I'm scared, and . . . and I want to go home."

"That's why we're here," Justin said in a soothing voice. He took the blanket and wrapped it tightly around her shoulders. "You're safe now. I promise. We'll have you home in no time, in your own bed, and you'll have medicine to make your head stop hurting. How does that sound?"

Andi regarded Justin warily. "Are you really my brother?"

Justin lifted her from the ground and hugged her close to his chest. "Of course I am, honey."

Andi leaned her head against Justin's shoulder. Although she didn't recognize this stranger, it felt good to be picked up and held by him. It felt *right*.

She closed her eyes. "Take me home."

Chapter Sixteen

STARTING OVER

A ndi opened her eyes to the sound of murmuring voices. She noticed that a warm, cozy bed had replaced the cold ground. The dreadful pounding in her head had been exchanged for a dull ache, which was bearable. A single lamp burned on a table, bathing the room in a soft yellow glow.

"Well, Dr. Weaver?"

Andi turned her head toward the voice. An attractive older woman stood in earnest conversation with a tall, gray-haired man. The woman's silver-streaked blond hair hung down her back in a loose braid. Her blue eyes searched the doctor's face for an answer.

"I'll be honest with you, Elizabeth," came the quiet reply. "A gunshot wound is always serious. I cleaned and stitched it up the best I could. Let's hope it doesn't become infected."

"What about her memory?"

The doctor sighed. "Amnesia's a funny thing. She could have lost her memory from the head injury or even from the emotional shock she's experienced." He shrugged his helplessness. "I have no idea which it is. Frankly, it wouldn't matter if I did. There's no treatment. Just give her lots of rest, good food, and plenty of love. Surround her with familiar things, and who knows? She could regain her memory tomorrow." He snapped his fingers. "Just like that."

"Is it possible she might never regain it?"

The doctor held up his hand. "Please, Elizabeth. One worry at a time. There's no sense borrowing trouble. You know what the Scriptures say: 'Sufficient unto the day is the evil thereof.'" He laid a hand gently on her arm. "You've had plenty of evil for one day, I think. Just thank God they found her at all."

The woman named Elizabeth nodded.

Dr. Weaver closed his bag and turned to go. "See that someone stays with her until she wakes up. I'll come by tomorrow afternoon." He patted her shoulder. "You need some rest."

"Thank you for coming by at such a late hour, John."

"Think nothing of it. We've seen Andrea through everything from croup to measles. With God's help, we'll see her through this too." He smiled. "I'll let myself out."

The woman turned back to Andi, who quickly shut her eyes. She didn't want anyone to know she was awake. She wasn't ready to talk to anybody, not even to this beautiful, sad-faced woman who must be her mother.

She felt the cool, tender touch of the woman's hand against her cheek and nearly jumped. Then the bed covers were tucked gently around her. A light kiss brushed across the bandage on her head.

"Andrea," the woman's soft voice whispered, "I know you can't hear me. Even if you could, you don't know me. But it's all right. When I learned you were gone, I cried out to the Lord and He brought you back this far. That's all that matters for now. I know He'll bring you the rest of the way in His own time."

After a pause, the voice continued. "Mr. Foster says you were brave—the bravest in the class. You saved Virginia's life. Of course, it doesn't mean much to you now, sweetheart, but in time you'll understand." Andi heard the rustling of paper. "I'll read aloud for a while. Perhaps the sound of my voice will trigger a memory somewhere."

Andi lay still, perfectly content. She would have listened to her mother's soothing voice for the rest of the night, but the warmth of the bed enveloped her, and she fell asleep.

"Well, young lady," Dr. Weaver boomed cheerfully, "it looks like you're on the mend." He dropped the soiled white cloth, which had served as a bandage for the past week, into the basin. "You won't be needing this any longer. No bleeding, no fever, no redness. Everything is coming along nicely. Patients like you make me feel good about my profession."

He squeezed Andi's arm and stood up from the bed. "You can get up and return to a few quiet activities. In another week or two, you'll be as good as new."

"Not quite," Andi said.

Dr. Weaver frowned. "Don't be impatient, Andrea. Give yourself time to remember."

Mother lowered herself onto the bed, where Andi sat propped against the headboard. She picked up one of her hands and held it between her own. "Sweetheart, do you remember anything about the accident? Anything at all?"

Andi grew quiet. She stared past her mother, past the doctor, and through the French doors leading outside to the balcony. Remembering was hard work. It was easier to let her mind wander to less important matters, like what she was having for supper tonight. She found herself doing that a lot lately.

"Andrea," Mother prompted.

"I remember the blood." Andi shivered. "I remember how much it hurt." She closed her eyes and drew a deep breath. "I remember a scruffy-looking man talking to me." She opened her eyes. "Sometimes I see him yelling at me, telling me to do something I don't want to do. I'm sitting on a horse. I remember him galloping away. I don't remember anything else."

"Well, that's something." Dr. Weaver winked his encouragement. He picked up his bag and turned to leave. "I'll drop by the beginning of next week to take out the stitches. If you need anything before then, just send word."

Mother nodded and rose from the bed. "I must see to supper, Andrea. We'd like you to join us downstairs tonight."

"Do I have to?" She didn't want to go downstairs. She didn't want to sit at the table and feel her sister's and brothers' pity. She could see it in their eyes and hear it in their forced attempts at cheerfulness.

"It will be our last supper as a family for a while. Chad and Mitch are heading out on roundup tomorrow to bring the stock down from the high country. It will be a couple of weeks before they return. We've missed you at meals, sweetheart."

Andi gave in. "All right."

Her mother blew her a kiss before she left the room. "You rest now. I'll send someone to fetch you when supper's ready."

Rest. Andi grimaced. *That's all I've been doing for days and days. So, why am I always tired?* She lay back against the pillows and stared at the ceiling. Within minutes, she was asleep.

"Andi?"

A quiet whisper brought her awake. She sat up, curious. Standing outside her door was a girl not much older than herself. She had huge brown eyes and black hair pulled tightly into two shiny braids.

"Who are you?" Andi asked.

"Rosa. My parents work for your family. So do I. *Mamá* would not let me talk to you until today, after the doctor left." She lowered her voice. "But many times I sneaked in while you were sleeping, to pray God might heal you." She broke into a beautiful smile. "And *gracias a Dios,* He heard my prayers."

Andi smiled. "Thank you." She patted the bed. "Sit down and visit with me awhile."

"Actually," Rosa said, sitting down on the bed and slipping into rapid Spanish, "the *señora* sent me up here to tell you it's almost suppertime. She thought maybe you'd like me to help you dress and show you the way to the dining room."

Rosa's expression was so hopeful that Andi consented. She allowed Rosa to pick out a dress and brush her hair. The girl was careful around the place where the bandage had been.

"There," Rosa announced a few minutes later. *"Mucho mejor."*

Andi studied her reflection in the mirror. She didn't think she looked much better. The dark-haired stranger staring back at her looked frightened and lost. The scattering of freckles across her nose stood out in sharp contrast to her pale face. There was no sparkle in her wide blue eyes.

She reached up and carefully pulled aside her hair. With her other hand, she traced the ugly row of stitches along the side of her head. The tiny black threads tickled her fingers. Andi shuddered and let her hair fall forward to hide the rough-looking gash. She knew right then she'd have a scar for life.

"When you return to school," Rosa said, "everyone will want to see it, *no?*" Her voice grew quiet when Andi didn't answer. *"Lo siento,"* she mumbled in apology.

"It's all right." Andi stood up. "I'd better go downstairs."

Rosa left Andi at the dining room doorway and disappeared toward the kitchen to help her mother.

"Well, young lady," Justin greeted her, hurrying to her side, "don't you look pretty tonight!" He led her to a place next to Melinda and pulled out the chair.

"We're having your favorite supper," Melinda said. "Can you guess what it is?"

Andi shook her head and sat down.

"Try," Mitch encouraged. "What's the first thing that comes to your mind when you think of food?"

"Fried chicken, mashed potatoes and gravy, and . . . biscuits and jam?"

"That's exactly right, Andi," Justin said with an encouraging wink. "You remembered."

Nila and Rosa appeared with the meal. Fried chicken it was, along with many things Andi had not guessed: a heaping platter of golden corn on the cob, a dish overflowing with green beans, and two pans of fresh peach cobbler.

A spark of hope raced through Andi at the sight. She smiled shyly at Justin and picked up her fork.

It was a little awkward talking to a roomful of strangers, but they were nice strangers, Andi decided. And the food was delicious. She only had to be polite and not spill her milk or do anything else to embarrass herself. Soon she would be allowed to return to the security of her room.

"Your friends miss you," Justin remarked, buttering a biscuit. "They paid a visit to my office this afternoon. They want to know when you're coming back to school."

Andi froze, a chicken leg halfway to her mouth. "Never."

"Never is a long time, Andrea," Mother said.

"Cory asked if he could come out to the ranch to see you," Justin continued as if his sister hadn't spoken. "I told him to wait a few more days."

"I don't want any visitors."

"Come on, Andi," Chad broke in. "Couldn't you just talk to Cory? Maybe you'll recognize him."

"No!" Andi slammed the drumstick onto her plate. "I'm not ready." She reached for her milk with a shaking hand and tipped it over.

The contents spilled across the table and into Mitch's lap. With a startled yelp, he sprang from his chair.

Andi burst into tears.

"This started out as a quiet, enjoyable supper together," Mother reminded her family. "Please do not spoil it."

"I'm sorry, Andi," Chad apologized. He flung his napkin in Mitch's direction. "I won't mention it again."

Andi wiped her eyes. She picked up her piece of chicken and pretended to listen while her brothers talked about the roundup for the rest of the meal. She looked at each family member, trying to remember them.

It was no use. When supper was over, they remained as much a group of strangers as they'd been since she received the injury.

Chapter Seventeen

A TIME TO REMEMBER

*P*lease!" *Andi pleaded. "I want to go home. We've come far enough. Please! Let me go home."*

A rough voice laughed. "Nothin' doin', little lady. As long as I've got you, nobody will dare follow me."

Andi felt anger and fear rise up inside. She curled her fingers tightly around her horse's mane and shouted at a scruffy-looking, dark-eyed stranger. "I'm leaving."

An iron grip closed around her arm and tried to yank her from her horse.

Andi screamed. "Let me go! Let me—"

"Andrea. Wake up." A firm voice cut through Andi's dream. Her mother had her by the shoulders, gently shaking her awake. "You're dreaming again," she said, lowering herself to her daughter's side.

Andi sat up and threw her arms around her mother, not caring if the woman was still a stranger. She took several deep breaths to still her pounding heart. Slowly, she relaxed as her mother gently stroked her hair and spoke soothing words.

"Another nightmare?"

Andi nodded.

"Can you tell me about it?"

"It was so real," Andi whispered. "So dreadful. I think I'm starting to remember." She shivered. "But I don't want these kinds of memories. I'd rather not remember at all."

"You don't mean that, sweetheart."

"I do. I'm having more and more bad dreams."

Just then, Justin poked his tousled head into the room. "Is everything all right in here?" He smiled at Andi, but he looked at their mother for the answer to his question.

"Another bad dream," Mother explained.

"Ah, I see."

Andi caught the concerned look that passed between them. She closed her eyes and sighed. *They know.* No matter how hard she tried to keep her worries to herself, Justin and Mother had figured out she was not getting better.

Except for her bad dreams, Andi had remembered nothing of importance in the three weeks since she had been found. Her family had gone to great lengths to help her regain her memory, but nothing seemed to work.

Just before heading out for the high country, Chad had shown Andi a big, dappled-gray stallion prancing around inside the corral. "When roundup's over, you and I are going to gentle Whirlwind," he promised, all smiles. "Now, how does that sound?"

Andi stared blankly at the horse. For some reason, Chad expected her to be excited by this offer. Why? She swallowed in uncertainty and mumbled an answer. When her brother's shoulders sagged and he walked away, she knew it was the wrong answer.

Would she ever remember her family? The ranch? *Anything?* Andi didn't even recognize Taffy, although she rode the mare every day. Melinda always went along.

Probably to keep me from getting lost or—

"Andi, did you hear me?"

Andi flinched, and her eyes flew open. She shook her head.

Justin smiled. "Why don't we head to the kitchen for a midnight snack?"

"I'm not hungry."

"Sure you are," Justin said. "We'll heat some chocolate and talk a bit." He turned to Mother. "I learned something important today. I wasn't sure when I should bring it up, but now seems like a good time."

"All right." Mother rose from the bed and held out her hand. "Come along, sweetheart. Let's find something to eat and see what your brother has to say."

Over cups of steaming chocolate and a plate of sugar cookies, Andi listened to Justin's discovery.

"Sheriff Tate dropped by my office today. He brought a telegram from down south that says Jed Hatton was captured." He paused.

"And?" Mother urged.

"They're bringing him back to Fresno by train. He should be here in a couple of days." Justin lowered his cup of chocolate. "Russ told me that Jed shot up a couple of deputies while trying to escape. That doesn't sound like an innocent man to me."

He let out a deep, regretful sigh. "How could I have been so wrong? If I hadn't believed in his innocence, I never would have defended him. He might have gotten a different sentence. Then he wouldn't have returned to town and—" He glanced at Andi, who was listening with interest.

"Don't do this to yourself, Justin," Mother said. "What's done is done. Just tell me why on earth the man's coming back to Fresno. I'd prefer to see him safely behind bars in San Quentin."

"When I heard about his capture, I asked if he could be brought here before going on to prison."

"Whatever for?"

"Because we can't go on like this, Mother. It's been three weeks and Andi's no better." Justin sighed. "I have an idea. It may not be a very good one, but it's worth a try. If Andi saw Jed, if she could hear him talk, something might trigger her memory and bring it back."

Andi gasped. This was not a good idea *at all*.

"You're so close, honey," Justin coaxed. "You're almost remembering."

"What if something goes wrong?" Mother asked. "What if talking to Jed pushes her memories deeper?"

"Well, it certainly can't get much worse. I say we should give it a try."

"Andrea, what do you think?" Mother asked. "Do you want to take a chance on remembering by confronting the man who hurt you?"

Andi bit her lip and stared at her cooling chocolate. The image of a dirty, unshaven face loomed up in front of her. She wanted to forget that face, not see it for real. She started to shake her head, but then chanced a look at her brother.

Justin's eyes were filled with deep regret and sorrow, as if he blamed himself for what had happened to her. Yet he always put on a cheerful face and tried to make her happy. Couldn't she do this one thing for him?

"I'm scared," she said.

Justin gave Andi's hand a squeeze. "I know you are, but he can't hurt you any longer. He's behind bars."

Andi let out a deep breath. She didn't want to do it, but she was so tired of looking at her family and seeing only strangers. *Help me do this thing, God,* she prayed. Then she nodded. "All right."

"Good girl." Justin broke into a smile. "I'll be with you the whole time. We'll see this through together."

"We've come to see Jed Hatton," Justin announced when he and Andi walked into the sheriff's office two days later.

"I hope you know what you're doing, Justin." The sheriff waved a greeting to Andi, who didn't return it. "He's not exactly in a cooperative mood back there. Are you sure this is a good idea?"

"No, I'm not sure it's a good idea. But it's the only idea I've had all month. Now c'mon, Russ, let me see him."

The sheriff opened the door that led to the jail cells. "Hatton," he called, "you've got visitors. It's your lawyer."

"He ain't my lawyer no more."

"He's visiting you just the same."

Justin and Andi stepped around the sheriff, and then Justin motioned Andi to stay where she was. She watched him walk down the cell-lined corridor.

Justin stopped in front of a cell. "It's good to see you alive, Jed."

The man snorted.

"It is. I really am glad to see you. Do you know why you've made the stop here in Fresno?"

"Nope. Don't care, neither."

"It's so you can clear your conscience before you head to prison."

"Huh? Don't talk in riddles."

Justin sighed. "All right, Jed. Here it is. I defended you in court. Got you a prison sentence instead of a noose. I did my best for you because I believed you were innocent. And I continued to believe, even when I heard you'd escaped. I wanted to help you by going after an appeal, but you wouldn't give me a chance."

He took a step forward and gripped the bars of the cell. "Instead, you repaid me by kidnapping my sister and leaving her to die out in the middle of nowhere."

Jed's voice dropped to a whisper. "She's *dead*?"

"No. We found her in time, no thanks to you." Justin shook his head. "You know, my brother Chad would love to get his hands on you for what you did. I'm tempted to let him, but he might have to stand in line. It won't take long before the good citizens of this town find out you're here."

"What do you want from me?" Jed growled.

Justin stepped back and let his hands drop to his sides. "I want you to help restore my sister's memory. She can't remember anything up to the day we found her. The gunshot wound to her head is the cause."

"Where do I come in?"

"Talk to her. Help her relive the last few minutes before her . . ." Justin paused. "*Accident.*"

"It *was* an accident," Jed said. "Just a warning shot to scare her into coming back. I never meant to hit her. When she fell off her horse, I brought her back to camp and tended her the best I could. But I was scared, lawyer. You don't know *how* scared. I figured you'd shoot me on sight, so I took off. I meant no harm to the girl. You gotta believe me."

"I'd like to believe you," Justin said. He turned and called, "Come here, honey."

Andi joined Justin in front of the cell. She looked up at Jed and felt herself fill with dread. The man behind these bars was clean-shaven, not scruffy and dirty like the face in her memory. His hair was combed neatly to the side.

"Do you recognize him?" Justin asked.

"I don't know."

"I sure remember you, little lady," Jed said. "I'm glad to learn you're all right. It was real scary seein' you lying there so still."

Andi shook her head and backed away. She might not recognize his face, but his voice struck a chord deep inside. She knew she'd heard it somewhere before. The brief image of a man looking up at her and talking flashed through her head. She winced. "No," she whispered.

Jed grinned. "You sure had a lot of pluck to sass me the way you did, 'specially when I was holdin' a gun on you. You were sittin' up on that horse all keen on runnin' off. Said your brothers were gonna catch me, and I'd hang. That wasn't nice, girl. You should've stuck with me. We'd have been over the border by now, and I would've let you go—more'n likely."

Andi looked at Justin, who motioned her to keep talking to Jed.

But she didn't want to. She'd heard enough of his voice. "Justin, it's not working. Can we go home now?" She turned away from the cell.

"Goin' somewhere, little lady?"

Jed's voice and the familiar words stopped Andi in her tracks. She caught her breath and whirled to face Jed. A chill raced up her spine. She'd heard those very words before. They had burned themselves into her mind.

An instant later, she saw the campsite in her mind—just like in her nightmares. Her heart beat faster. A picture formed in her head of Jed sitting against a tree, gun raised. Suddenly, it was crystal clear. Andi knew that the words she spoke next, she had spoken before.

"I'm going home!" she cried.

Andi's memory returned in such a flood that she staggered backward. Justin caught her, but she pushed away from him and walked up to the bars of Jed's cell. "I remember!" she shouted. "I remember *everything*. Why did you shoot me? I only wanted to go home, and you wouldn't let me."

She whipped around to face Justin and the sheriff. "I remember something else too. He told me he really did kill Mr. Slater. He did it for the gold dust."

Jed whistled. "You sure got your memory back in a hurry, girl."

Andi ignored him. She threw her arms around Justin. "I know you, Justin. I really do." She didn't know whether to laugh or cry, so she did both. Happy tears poured down her face. She brushed them away and hugged her brother tighter. She heard him whisper, "Thank God."

Sheriff Tate echoed Justin's words. "Thank God is right. It's been a long three weeks for everyone." Tears glistened in his eyes. "It's good to have you back, Andi," he said solemnly, reaching out his hand.

Andi took the sheriff's large, calloused hand and squeezed it. "Thank you, Sheriff. I'm awfully glad to *be* back."

"Don't hear nobody thankin' *me*," Jed grumbled.

Justin and the sheriff escorted Andi down the hall and back into the office.

"So," Sheriff Tate said, locking the corridor door. "Now that you've got your memory back, what's the first thing you're going to do?"

Andi's joy bubbled over. "I'm going to hug my mother and my sister, and then I'm going to hug Taffy." There were so many things Andi wanted to do that she started talking faster. "When Chad and Mitch get back from roundup, I'll hug them too. And *then*"—she laughed—"I'm going to hold Chad to his promise to let me help gentle Whirlwind."

"That's all well and good," Justin said. "But they won't be home for another week. Until then, you are going back to school."

"*School?* No, Justin! I'm not ready to—"

"If you're up to helping gentle Whirlwind, then you're more than ready to go back to school tomorrow."

"Tomorrow?" Andi's joy bubble burst. She slumped.

But Justin was right. She had to go back to school eventually, so she might as well go tomorrow and get it over with.

Chapter Eighteen

BACK TO SCHOOL

"I feel like I've swallowed a thousand butterflies," Andi said when she saw the schoolhouse the following morning. "I don't want to do this."

Justin smiled. "After all you've been through, how scary can walking into a roomful of your classmates be?"

"Plenty scary." Andi shivered. "By now they've most likely read the *Expositor's* fanciful account of what happened. I'll have to listen to an earful of questions, when all I want is to forget the whole thing."

"I know," Justin agreed. "But Fresno's a small town. Saving Virginia's life is big news. Better learn to accept the attention gracefully."

Andi squirmed. Easier said than done.

Justin brought the buggy to a standstill near the schoolyard and climbed out. "Come on. It won't be as hard as you think. I promise."

Andi had no choice but to accept Justin's help down and leave the security of the buggy. She clasped Rosa's hand. "Let's slip into the schoolhouse before anybody sees us," she whispered.

Rosa laughed. "*¡Eso es imposible!*"

Andi realized how impossible it was as soon as she stepped foot in the schoolyard. It was crowded with students, all laughing and running and waiting for the first bell to ring. She looked around with the eyes of an outsider. How strange it felt!

Some of the little boys were involved in a rousing game of tug-of-war. Cory and the older boys were deep in conference around the water barrel near the side of the building. One of the boys put a small object into the dipper. A frog, no doubt. A small grin cracked Andi's face. She would make sure she didn't go after the first drink at recess.

She glanced at the small clusters of girls scattered across the yard. The primary girls were jumping rope and playing as loudly as the little boys. They clasped their arms around each other and waited for their turns.

The oldest girls, with their ankle-length skirts and their hair carefully pinned up, whispered among themselves near the steps. The girls nearest Andi's age stood by the old oak tree, taking turns on the swing hanging from a high, thick branch.

Andi noticed Virginia Foster watching the group from a distance. The girl took a few halting steps toward the swing, hesitated, and turned back. Then she saw Andi, and her eyes widened in surprise. Picking up her skirt, she clattered up the porch steps and disappeared into the schoolhouse.

"What in the world?" Andi wondered aloud.

A shout prevented her from following Virginia into the building. "Andi!" Rachel leaped from the swing. "You're back!"

The children swarmed around Andi. To her surprise, her uneasiness melted away at the sound of her classmates welcoming her back to school—just as Justin had promised. In response to her friends' eager questions, she found herself sharing not only her story, but also showing off her scar.

The little girls covered their mouths and made faces at the sight. *Oohs* and *aahs* of admiration burst from the older boys and girls. Even the school bully, Johnny Wilson, seemed impressed.

"I've gotta hand it to you, Andi," he admitted. "You've got plenty of gumption, if nothing else."

"You should've been here when Mr. Foster came to," Maggie said.

"He nearly went mad with fear when he found out you were gone. I think he figured your family was going to blame him for what happened."

Jack Goodwin laughed. "Well, one good thing's come from all this. Mr. Foster's sure been a lot nicer these past few weeks. Nobody but Johnny's been thrashed for days."

Everyone laughed—except Johnny.

The first bell rang, breaking up the curious crowd and calling them to class.

Cory hung back and plucked Andi's sleeve. "I just thought of something. You could've made heaps of money."

"What are you talking about?"

"You could have charged the kids to let them look at your gunshot scar. You know, sort of like a peep show—a penny a peek."

"Cory, that's awful!" Then she noticed his mischievous grin and started laughing.

By the time Andi entered the classroom, she felt completely at ease. She headed for the desk she shared with Rosa and slipped into her seat. Gently, she brushed her palm across the top of her desk and smiled. It felt good to be back. It really did. She lifted the lid and reached for her books. Her hand curled around a long, wriggling shape.

Andi jerked her hand back. "There's something in my desk," she told Rosa. Carefully, she peeked under the lid. A pair of small beady eyes stared back. A tongue lashed out.

"Welcome back," Cory whispered over her shoulder. "It's only Clyde."

Andi slammed the desktop shut and whirled on Cory. "I'm gonna wrap this snake around your neck and—"

"School is in session, Miss Carter."

Andi sat up straight and turned around. "Yes, sir." She waited for the schoolmaster to scold her or order her to the front of the class to whack her palms for talking after the tardy bell rang.

Mr. Foster did neither. He just looked at her.

Andi squirmed. "Am I in trouble?"

"No, Miss Carter." He came around to the front of his desk and crossed his arms over his chest. "Not this time."

Andi didn't know what to think. Why was he looking at her so keenly?

"It's good to see you're well enough to attend school," Mr. Foster said at last. He held up his hand to prevent Andi from replying. With his other hand he picked up a folded newspaper from his desk. "It is not my intention to embarrass you," he said, "but I would like to read the article that appeared in the *Expositor* for the benefit of the class."

Andi stared at her desktop. She was pretty sure everybody in class had already seen the story. "Please don't," she whispered.

Mr. Foster read it anyway. Once more Andi had to listen to the account of her ". . . dangerous but courageous decision to leave the safety of her classroom and journey into the unknown to save the life of a schoolmate . . ."

Thankfully, it was short.

He put down the paper. "It's quite a different story from the one the paper ran several weeks ago."

A hard knot settled in Andi's stomach. Would he *never* forgive her for almost trampling him? Her delight in returning to school began to dissolve.

Mr. Foster continued. "I admit we've had our differences, Miss Carter. You do not easily conform to the rules of propriety, and it has brought you no end of trouble this term." He paused and took a deep breath. "However, your willingness to take my daughter's place made me realize that what I interpreted as defiance and brashness was in reality courage and strength of character. I can never repay you for what you did for my family. I can only thank you from the bottom of my heart."

His expression twisted into an unexpected smile. "What I'm trying to say is, I'm proud to have you as my student, Andrea Carter. Welcome back."

The knot in Andi's stomach melted away, replaced by a warm glow. She returned Mr. Foster's smile. "Thank you, sir." Now, if only he'd give the day's assignments and move on. She'd had about all the attention she could stomach.

Mr. Foster wasn't finished. "Miss Foster, you may come forward at this time."

Virginia rose from her seat and glided up the aisle to the front of the classroom. Slowly she turned around, clasped her small hands in front of her skirt, and faced Andi. She looked pale, but when she opened her mouth, her words came out clear and steady.

"I've been practicing what I'm going to say for days, ever since I woke up and learned you'd left the classroom with that outlaw. It should have been me. It *would* have been me if you hadn't done what you did." She swallowed. "Father says you saved my life. I want to say thank you."

Andi waited. Would Virginia also make things right about the stallion and apologize for the lies she'd told? When no more words came, Andi said, "You're welcome."

Virginia gave Andi a slight nod, curtsied to her father, and started for her seat.

Mr. Foster frowned, as though Virginia's words were not exactly what he had expected. "Is that all, Miss Foster? You've nothing to add?"

Virginia stopped. She gave her father a puzzled look. "I don't think so, sir."

Mr. Foster grunted. "What about your part in the scuffle a few weeks back?"

"Oh!" Virginia's pale cheeks turned pink. "Of course it was wrong of me to slap you, Andrea," she said. "My mother says a lady *never* resorts to physical displays of anger. I apologize."

"And the lying?" Mr. Foster's voice was firm.

"Father!"

"All of it, daughter."

Virginia sighed. "I cannot ride a horse. I'm sorry I led you to believe that I could." She bowed her head and shuffled back to her seat.

Poor Virginia, Andi thought. *It must be hard admitting her faults in front of her father and the entire class.*

Andi caught Virginia's skirt when she passed her desk. "It's all right," she whispered. "I forgive you. And if you like, I can teach you how to ride."

Virginia paused. "Thank you." Then she raised her head and smiled at Andi. A tear trickled down her cheek. "Thank you very much."

This time Andi knew she meant it.

Mr. Foster reached for the classroom Bible.

Of course, Andi *should* have been listening to the Scripture reading. It was all about the Golden Rule. "Such a fitting topic for this morning," the teacher commented between verses.

But Andi's mind was not on the inspiring words the teacher was reading. All she could think was, *What am I going to do about Cory's snake?*

A literature unit study guide with enrichment activities is available for *Andrea Carter and the Dangerous Decision* as a free download at www.CircleCAdventures.com.

Contact Susan K. Marlow at susankmarlow@kregel.com.